DHAMPIRICA

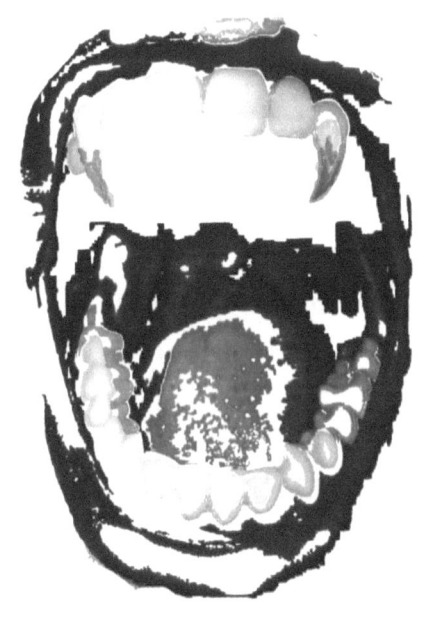

Also by W.J. Cherf

The Manuscripts of the Richards' Trust

Bow Tie

Recovery

Children of Ptah

Imhotep

Maat-ka-re. Memoires of a Time Traveler

The Adventures of J.J. Stone

The First Soul

The Lictor of Magic

I Am The Storm

Adventures in Paranormal Archaeology

The Magician's Tomb

Netherworld's Gate

DHAMPIRICA

ADVENTURES IN PARANORMAL ARCHAEOLOGY III

BY

W.J. CHERF

FBP

FOXBAT PUBLISHING

Foxbat Publishing
ISBN: 978-1-7329779-0-7

Dhampir, noun, masc. **-ica**, fem. 1) Progeny of a male vampire and human female. 2) Vampire hunter. Etymology: from Albanian, *dham* (teeth) and *pirë* (to drink). Serbian *vampijerović, vampirović,* and *vampirić.* See Bosnian *lampijerović,* with the literal meaning of "vampire's son." *Wikipedia.*

DEDICATION

While this is hardly my first rodeo, I nonetheless remain deeply indebted to those who offer their invaluable criticism—both good and bad. The process of storytelling is not an easy one. It, frankly, is more a test of one's creativity and stubborn discipline, then anything else. Still, I enjoy the process and that's what counts.

To my copy editor, Stephanie, thank you always and forever for your careful attention and helpful suggestions. As usual, you have transformed a sow's ear into a silk purse.

My Sweet Sue is first and last a Star Trek nerd if there ever was one. I know that you don't always like what I write, but you slog through the pages and ferret out my blunders. As I have said so many times before, getting you to smile just once is all that really matters.

PART I: ORIGINS

CHAPTER 1

If a fleeting whiff of perfume can trigger memories of long-lost passion and lust for mortals, then for *others*, the distinct bouquet of fresh blood can enliven far more primal instincts.

Atop the lofty heights of a rugged mountainside an apex predator peered down in rapt anticipation. His name was Sigmund. Hunger ruled him as the tall dark figure scanned the majestic intermontane view. For far below lay neatly cultivated fields, fruit groves, and modest habitations. Meandering snake-like wisps of smoke rose from several cooking fires.

"Ah, the possibilities," he grunted, in a guttural northern European tongue.

Sigmund could not remember, much less count, how many centuries, lo' millennia, he had been in existence. Old memories of barren tundra, cold and snow, had driven him south into warmer climes. Even his near-mythic Germanic name was a recent fiction, the latest in a long line.

Then, like a peal of thunder, this predator's hypersensitive nose caught an errant scent that jarred its senses. The powerfully sweet aroma beckoned. Unbidden, nostrils flared to parse the delicious scent, fortified with youthful vibrancy. Turning his head this way and that, Sigmund divined the direction of the wind-borne source. Fully fixated and eyes dilated, the hunter recklessly began its descent, leaping down from crag to boulder with preternatural ease. Along the way, a yearning hunger made his mouth water. Two fangs, extending in excited anticipation, pricked his heavily scarred lower lip. Already dark eyes dilated wider as the pace quickened. Down the mountain's final scree he flitted like a shadow across a mirror. Through the tree line of the upland forest Sigmund bounded like a deer until it reached the rich alluvial floor of the valley. Panting, alive, and invigorated by the hunt, the vampire began its stalk.

* * *

A young woman suffering her first pangs of womanhood, struggled with her hand-held scythe amid the stands of ripe wheat. Usually she worked in a low waddling squat, but today she knelt quietly groaning. Inching forward on her knees, the farm maid took another low pass with her well-muscled right arm. The crude tool—made of antler bone and sharp obsidian microliths—easily cleaved away a handful of stalks. These she stacked neatly to the side in crisscrossing piles of four. Looking back over her shoulder she puffed away at an errant lock of wavy dark-brown hair, and smiled at the progress made since that dewy sunrise. She knew that her father would be proud.

The day had turned late beneath a powder-blue sky dappled with fluffy clouds, but Rovena, tired, doggedly continued with her harvesting. The last swing taxed her, so she sat up on her knees to catch a breath. Cramping badly, she grunted loudly, and bent over again. Lances of pain shot through her stomach. Gritting her teeth, Rovena brushed back another lock of hair, and took another pass through the tawny sheaths. Dried salt painted the sides of her unwrinkled oval face, one beautiful beyond compare. Gold-flecked gray eyes tried to see past the stinging salt clinging to her long black lashes. She pursed her rosebud lips in pain.

Presently, a cooling shadow shaded her. Looking up, Rovena saw a tall stranger standing over her. She took him in. Lean of face, he wore an unusual broad-brimmed leather hat, linen robes, and a hooded cloak of the well-to-do. He was shod with stout leather foot coverings that strapped up his ankles and calves. His clean-shaven face was long and triangular. Dark eyes framed a narrow beak-like nose. A simple leather throng gathered long curly black hair at the nape of his neck. His skin was the golden color of ripe wheat.

The stranger paused over her, lifted his head, and scented the air. Then he smiled down at the farm maid in a warm, inviting way. "You, who labors so hard while under such distress," he said with oddly accented words. "Where is your father?" He asked with authority as his hands rode upon narrow hips. The easy pose set off his broad, oxen-like shoulders. But before Rovena could answer, he continued.

"Or has he abandoned you like a common field slave?" he concluded with an imperious rise of his chin.

In response, Rovena sat up to look about, and discovered with surprise that she had indeed been abandoned in the field. All the others had left for home, even the gleaners. Noting the sun was about to disappear behind the valley's western mountain, Rovena said, "I must have been day-dreaming, Noble One. My father can be found either at our home or at the mill over there," she said smiling, while shading her eyes and pointing off toward the west.

Dark eyes slowly scanned in that direction. Then the stranger cryptically said, "Verily, Providence has indeed smiled upon me today."

Looking down again at the kneeing farm maid, "I am called Sigmund. What is your name child?"

"Rovena, Noble One."

"Rovena … what an interesting name. Do you know its meaning?"

"No, Noble One. All I know is that my parents didn't name me. An old high priestess did."

"Ah, a priestess you say. How appropriate. Well child, your name means 'sacred lance' in a very old tongue."

At that moment a dusky dark shadow fell across the valley as the setting sun occluded behind the mountain. The air chilled. The song of birds and insects stilled. Sigmund smiled and removed his broad brimmed hat. It fell to the ground.

Before Rovena could blink, the now hatless nobleman knelt before her, pushed her back to the ground, and raised her blood-stained lower garment. Gasping in surprise, Rovena watched as the man plunged his head between her thighs and began licking at her womanhood.

Shocked at the swift and audacious act, Rovena squealed and struggled to wriggle free, but failed to escape Sigmund's powerful grasp. With ever-widening eyes, the virgin girl gasped wide-eyed at the exquisite sensations that beat against her loins like waves on a seashore. In a matter of moments however, Rovena ceased to struggle, and instead began to breathe heavily. In nearing ecstasy, she squirmed this way and that, her thighs held wide in total surrender. She entangled her fingers in his sweaty hair, and pulled his head to her. Suddenly, the stranger broke free, rose up, and in a storm of lust, plunged himself deeply into her. Soon his moans matched hers in rhythm and urgency.

When the farm maid gasped in full release, only then did she focus upon the stranger's blood stained lips, his open, panting mouth, and his two eye teeth that seemed to be lengthening. At that frightening vision she jerked in fear and tried to break free again, but he continued to thrust on and on. Reaching his climax, the stranger bellowed like a bull. Withdrawing, he bent forward and held her shoulders down, pinning them firmly against the rich, fertile earth.

"This time, my beautiful Rovena, I will spare you. Next time, however, you may not be so lucky." And like a ghost, Sigmund vanished into the gathering darkness.

Ashamed, yet curiously warmed by the frightening nobleman's attentions, Rovena gathered herself, retrieved her hand sickle and water jug, and made for home. When she arrived, the young woman found everyone sitting around the central fire pit, all deeply engrossed in their evening meal. Her father, seeing the front of his daughter's blood-stained garment, eyed his wife and notched his chin. The wife immediately rose and took her eldest daughter outside to the well head.

"Strip," she commanded.

Rovena did.

"When did your womanhood begin to weep?"

"Only this morning."

"Hrmph."

"Wash yourself," she commanded, as she extended a full bucket of the well's icy clear water. This Rovena did, but while she performed her ablutions, her mother noticed a whitish streak of mucous amidst the blood.

"Who did you lie with?" she pointedly accused.

"No one mother," Rovena guiltily blushed.

"You lie! His seed runs down your leg. Who was it? That adventurous potter's son?"

"No mother."

"Then, who was it?"

"A tall stranger, a nobleman, dressed in fine clothes."

This rich fantasy earned Rovena a slap across the face that knocked her to the ground.

"Liar!"

"Who did you lie with?"

The young woman shook her head in defiance. "I am no liar, mother. It was a tall nobleman."

"More lies!"

"He is called Sigmund," Rovena said with a surprising amount of pride and defiance.

That retort resulted in a swift kick to the stomach. Rovena buckled over, gasping in pain.

"Thoroughly clean your clothes and yourself. You sicken me. Sleep with the animals! And try not to couple with any of them!"

And so began Rovena's new life, one now filled with distrust and suspicion, and with parents who practically disowned her. Her father wouldn't even speak to her as his disappointment ran so deep.

* * *

The day following the nobleman's unwanted visit, a middle-aged farmer with graying temples sat in his mill before a silent grinding stone. He wore a dull look on his face.

"What's on your mind my husband?"

"Our daughter, what else? It seems that ever since that prying priestess made her visit after her birth, Rovena has been cursed."

"Do you really believe that?" the wife chided.

"Rovena has always been your favorite."

"It all began with that priestess' insistence on her birth name. That, from the very start, troubled me."

"Strange, my husband, I remember you were quite pleased at the time with the priestess' attention."

"Such a fine young girl, so strong and healthy, how could such a thing befall her?"

A knowing smile. "My husband, do you not remember how you wooed me that first night?"

A growling grumble emanated from his chest.

"But with a passing nobleman of all things. Who is this man? That is what vexes me. Where is he to care for our daughter? Take responsibility for his rash actions?"

"Gone like the summer wind I suspect," the wife concluded with her hands on hips.

To this her husband grunted his displeasure. "Well, I suppose that I should make an effort to find out about this Sigmund. Tomorrow I will go to the market and make inquiries about him. Is there anything needful for me to fetch?"

After some thought, "Salt, my husband. I have much to put up for the winter."

*   *   *

Along the mountain valley's western margin stood a hamlet made up of four rugged structures arranged in a crude circle. Along one side the seasonal tented stalls of traders flapped and snapped noisily in the breeze, while opposite, a rocky whitewater stream gurgled. Through its center ran an earthen track that connected the valley with the encircling snow-covered heights. Depending upon the season, nature could quickly transform this way into either a muddy quagmire or dusty track.

Constructed of hand-hewn pine and hardwoods, the four buildings represented a considerable investment, measured in generations of toil, by several families of the valley. They in turn provided the essentials of valley existence: grain milling, pottery and beer-making, leather crafts and smithing, and the baking of breads and sweet cakes. This was a simpler time, long before the fortunes of the hamlet would wax and wane to eventually form an ancient town with stout stone walls.

By necessity the four structures represented intimately intertwined occupations. The miller's house with its ever-creaking waterwheel was connected to the baker's by a covered walkway that prevented the freshly ground flour from getting wet from rain or snow. The brewer depended upon the baker's yeast for its highly carbonated brews and the leather maker's goatskin bags for its intoxicating honey-laced milk fermentations. All depended upon the potter for their many cooking pots, storage jars, and sundry jugs and beer juglets. As for the smithy, little truly was made at its forge. The expense of raw ore had become prohibitive. Consequently, much was repaired by shrewd and ever more inventive means.

Such was this Bronze Age hamlet located in southeastern France. It was a place of few secrets, but much gossip and speculation. To call a gathering, all one had to do was strike "the conversation pole" erected in the hamlet's center twice with its "calling stick" that hung from a thick leather throng.

This particular morning, Rovena's father did so with a heavy heart. He did not have to wait long before seven men joined him at the conversation pole.

"Miller," the baker inquired, "what caused you to take me from my dough?" said the stocky man with flour dusting his forearms and tunic. "Be quick with your words, as it is fast arising."

"Your breads are always 'fast arising,' unless it is you who calls us together baker," the miller snapped back.

"Yet, here is my question neighbors. Has anyone

recently seen a tall and dark-haired nobleman passing through our lands recently? He wears a hooded cape and broad-brimmed leather hat."

"Does this nobleman perchance have a name?" the smithy asked.

After a moment of hesitation, the miller nervously provided, "Sigmund."

Silence fell among the seven at hearing the strange foreign name, accompanied by several shaking heads.

Several quick glances were exchanged, however, the smithy finally admitted sadly, "A day ago, my prized goat was killed by something. I was fattening it up for our winter solstice sacrifice."

"The fine white one with black ears?" the brewer asked with raised eyebrows.

"Yes, that is the one."

More head shakes in dismay at the awkward, if not portentous news of their lost sacrificial offering.

"Killed 'by something' you say?" the baker broke the mood as he nervously rubbed at some dough stuck under his fingernails.

"Yes," the smithy said. "Whatever it was, it drained the goat of all of its blood. Then brutally tore out its livers. I have never before seen such a monstrous thing done to an animal."

"Indeed, nor I," said the leather craftsman, now looking directly at the miller, seeking his eyes for some inkling of meaning.

"So miller, why pose this odd question?" the potter challenged. "Perchance, did *you* lose something of value as well?"

At this the miller with eyes suddenly wide and insane, lunged for the potter, but was restrained by the others.

"Miller, for someone who is usually of such a calm demeanor, clearly, I have somehow found a sore spot."

Turning to the smithy, the leather craftsman pointedly asked. "What did you do with your ravaged goat?"

"I destroyed it by fire."

"Ah, so you did not taste one morsel of its succulent flesh?" the leather craftsman asked.

"Not one, though I was sorely tempted."

"Why did you not give in to the temptation?"

"Because whatever killed it must be some sort of a monster, something unclean. I judged my prize goat defiled, maybe even cursed. To eat of its flesh …" the smithy just grimaced and shook his head.

The leather craftsman now looked at the miller and what he saw was sheer, wide-eyed terror. "I agree with you smithy. Whatever took your prize goat must be a monster. And, as we all well know, whatever a monster touches is at the very least defiled. At the worst … cursed."

Head down while fussing with his ornate belt, the leather craftsman openly confronted the miller. "So, what did you lose to this nobleman called Sigmund? What thing of great value?"

The question caused the miller to hang his head. Tears ran freely. He snorted as they dropped off his nose. His heavily callused hand wiped away at them.

"This is about the fair Rovena, is it not, miller?" the potter guessed as he rubbed clay from his hands.

Silence was the miller's answer. Now with red-rimmed eyes, he turned away from the conversation post and returned to his mill with all thought of purchasing some salt from the baker forgotten.

As for the six who remained, knowing looks were exchanged, several of them openly lecherous.

After the evening meal, the young woman's father and mother had a conversation and decided that the daughter was defiled and selfish. Defiled by the nobleman Sigmund and selfish because her father's plans for a strategic marriage with the potter's son had been dashed.

*   *   *

Just before dawn the next day, Rovena's father went to the household's animal pen to awaken his daughter. Before doing so, he took a moment and looked around. The pen smelled different—fresher, cleaner. He had never before seen it so neat and well-swept. A pang of regret stabbed his heart as he gazed down upon her sleeping form nestled in a straw nest. His voice broke when he said, "Rovena, wake up," with a gentle shake of her shoulder.

"Father?"

"Take this bundle and leave before first light. Perhaps you can find a home in the next valley."

"But, but …"

"Shake the sleep from your head my beautiful Rovena. Go! Go now before the dawn arrives!"

"But, but …"

"Move quickly my sweet one! Others suspect that you are the carrier of an evil spawn! Don't let them find you!"

*   *   *

Rovena did as she was told and immediately left. With tears flooding down her face, the young woman obeyed her father and disappeared into the darkness. As she neared the surrounding forest that ringed the valley, Rovena finally dared to peer within the bundle that her father had provided. In the predawn light, she found within her mother's worn flax robe—generous in size and warm, two loaves of bread, and two dried fish.

Just as dawn broke upon the vale, the young woman stood at the forest's edge, a dark and densely-leafed curtain that no doubt hid many things. With a final glance over her shoulder Rovena found she could no longer see home, only a dark wisp of its cooking fire. Without another thought, she turned, parted several bushes, and entered the green gloom.

On her own, Rovena began the process of eking out an existence within the forested margins of the valley. That first day she took shelter in a small cave, hoarded her bundle, and started gathering food from nature's bounty of berries and nuts. One bad experience with mushrooms, however, caused Rovena to swear off them entirely.

In no time, the former farm maid learned how to leave no trace of her passage, breaking no twigs, disturbing no moss, while walking barefoot upon tree roots, rocks, and firm soils.

But by the time the moon cycled once, the young

woman, who suspected, now knew for sure. Her womanhood had not wept. The awful pains had not returned. Now her breasts had become tender. She now carried a child. The farm maid made a plan, long before she began to show.

She now had to think ahead as well. When Rovena came across a flowering blue flax clump that grew in a forest glade, she began gathering them up. From these fibers she would fashion garments not only to cover her swelling form, but also to clothe her for the coming winter—perhaps even to fashion some foot coverings. Her mother had taught her well.

*   *   *

In an often visited verdant and idyllic forest setting that overlooked a crystalline mountain stream teaming with trout, Rovena came across a hunched and arthritic woman who was settled upon a fallen, moss-covered log. This mildly irritated her as that spot was precisely her favorite place to sit in the sun's rays. The old woman's long gray-white tresses were colorfully braided with wild flowers. She nibbled on fresh bread, cheese, and roasted garlic, all arranged with an inviting purpose around her. All of this Rovena observed from her concealment behind a massive gnarled tree.

After some moments, the priestess casually looked up from her picnic meal and called out to the surrounding forest, "Come out, young one, and eat. I have plenty for the two of us."

Hesitant, the sight and smell of fresh bread made Rovena's stomach growl loudly, too much so.

"See, young one. Even your stomach agrees. Come forth and silence it."

Still unsure, Rovena silently approached from behind, constantly looking this way and that, expecting an ambush of some kind. After all, her father had warned her that others were fearful of her and the child that she carried.

Remaining quite still, the priestess called out again. "Why must such a beautiful woman stalk an old crone like me like a hungry wolf? I can assure you that my old bones carry little flesh, certainly, very little marrow."

Approaching silently from her hiding place, Rovena finally confronted the seated woman. What she beheld was graceful frailty, deep life lines, olive-colored skin, and shockingly intense light blue eyes. In short, she was a beautiful woman—grown old beyond estimation. "How do you know all of these things?" Rovena challenged.

"Ah, there you are! Greetings young one, I am called Hermonia. That makes you …" she said pointing, "Rovena. Yes?" she queried while extending a large portion of rough bread with a hearty crust.

"How …?" Rovena asked, snatching away the offering.

"Why, I named you child. How could I not know of it?"

Rovena took a bite. The bread tasted beyond delicious. Again her stomach agreed.

"You named me?"

"Yes, it is my duty within my religious order to do such things."

The young woman's eyes widened at the revelation.

"Have you ever fished here before?" the old priestess conversationally added. Hearing no answer, she continued.

"Well, I find these speckled ones, once baked over a fire, wonderfully tasty. Do you know how to do that?"

Rovena had already wolfed down all of her bread. "No, Honorable Hermonia, I do not."

"Ah, then child, watch and learn."

The priestess rose and quietly approached the gurgling stream taking care not to throw her shadow across its surface. Squatting down, she slowly revealed a thin pale arm from under her robe, and waited. Her lips moved silently. Soon, a fish approached within her reach. The priestess nodded to the fish in acknowledgement and with surprising speed, gripped the fish from behind its gills and lifted it clear of the stream. Dropping it in the tall green grass, the victim jumped and squirmed while the priestess refocused upon the stream, murmuring again to it.

In all three fish were captured and gutted swiftly by the priestess with a small knife that she produced from a hidden fold. The entrails, she carefully examined.

"Rovena, note these," she said, pointing with her delicate finger. "All are pink, healthy, and without stain. Never eat anything from the forest or stream that is putrefied. Also, note this cut that I have made along the length of both sides of the fish's spine."

"Why did you do that, Honorable One?"

"You will soon see. Now, fetch me three thin straight green sticks, each twice the fishes' length, and strip off their bark. I will make us a small fire."

When Rovena returned with her prepared sticks, she found the priestess squatting before a fine cooking fire of whitened coals. As Hermonia mounted each of the fish on their sticks, she chatted on.

"Rovena, we have much to discuss. Not so much about the cooking of fish, but rather about the future of the child that you carry."

"Oh…" Rovena reacted again in surprise at the old woman's knowledge.

Seeing the young woman's surprise, the priestess smiled warmly. "Indeed. While you carry your child well, you must know that it is hardly cursed, but instead is really quite special. Some would even say … blessed." This good news caused Rovena's heart to warm with a mother's pride. "Regardless, it must be cared for and raised in the proper way."

The fish near the fire began to sizzle, their aroma enticing. The priestess reached down to turn their sticks.

Rovena finally found her tongue. "How so, Honorable One I mean, about my child?"

"Its father is a horrible *thing* named Sigmund. Is that not so?" the priestess asked flatly.

"How…?"

Hermonia waved her hand brushing aside the question. "Sigmund is a monster. Always has been since his unfortunate creation," the priestess stated with passionate eyes. Now pointing, "But you know this truth as well as I. He and his kind must not be allowed to walk the earth. They all must be hunted down and destroyed."

Again she turned the fish-ladened sticks. Their skins had begun to crisp from the heat. Rovena saw they had begun to curl away from where the old priestess had sliced them.

Rovena briefly entertained a thought to leave the old one to her cooking, but her groaning stomach frankly prevented her from doing so.

Glancing at her knowingly, "I would not leave quite yet fair one. Firstly, you now have to eat for two—never forget that. Gorge yourself upon the flesh of rabbit, squirrel, fish, and deer. Your child dearly needs it. Village food is no longer for you. Secondly, you still do not know *what* your baby is, and more importantly, *why* it must survive."

"Then tell me, Honorable Hermonia," Rovena eagerly said as she rearranged herself in the moss and grass before her, "What *is* my child?"

Hermonia smiled broadly, for the first time revealing a set of perfectly white teeth, something Rovena had never before seen. "Most gladly. Your child, Rovena, is the rare product of the unliving, and you, a mortal female. Such a coupling makes your child a *dhampir*, or if a female child, a *dhampirica*."

She paused to turn the browning fish, which now sizzled in their own fat with their skins crisping nicely.

"Such offspring are a boon to mortal society as they are natural monster hunters, and their killers. At birth, they are endowed with senses far greater than mere mortals. These they need for the hunt and their survival against the unliving and their unsavory familiars."

"How do you know these things, Honorable One?"

"Because I have been waiting patiently to train our valley's next *dhampir*. You see, it is my purpose within my order. Sadly, I can no more perform this task alone. I have become old. I need help. Will you, Rovena, undertake this task? Will you help your child to survive and learn the many ways of the dhampir?"

Rovena nodded quickly, so quickly in fact that her sudden agreement surprised her.

"Good. I am pleased. I frankly was not sure you would. Not every mother loves her child. That tells me that you already love yours, and love, my dear Rovena, means much. There is not enough of it in this world. By the way, you have much to learn about the ways of fishing, the trapping of small animals, and the gathering of bird eggs, honey, berries, and nuts. All these I will gladly teach you."

*   *   *

Within the span of several weeks, the young woman named Rovena learned much from the priestess Hermonia about survival in the forest. She mastered the gentle enchantment spell for catching fish, another for starting a fire, and still another for concealment from predators and man. Her wizened teacher said she had much more to learn. The priestess explained the local herbs, their uses, what kinds of mushroom to eat and which not, and the other natural medicines that occurred seemingly everywhere underfoot.

Unlike Rovena's fearful parents and the superstitious villagers, the priestess Hermonia understood what happened to the young woman and what it meant for their valley—the potential for future protection from the undead and their minions. As a consequence, Hermonia's avowed purpose was to make sure the young woman's baby survived, come what may.

*   *   *

Just before the coming winter, Hermonia surprised Rovena by offering to take in the now very pregnant young woman. Against all the usual cycles of nature,

Rovena's hybrid child grew at a furious rate. While Hermonia knew of this, the priestess instead explained to Rovena that she needed a strong back to make it through the harsh season—clearly a half-truth.

Grateful beyond words, Rovena readily accepted the old woman's hospitality and none too soon. For by the early spring, she experienced a swift birth of a healthy baby girl—born a full three months early. Hermonia insisted on naming the babe Astra.

"While you nurse your child Rovena, it is very important that you continue to eat the flesh of rabbit and squirrel. But even more critical during this time, you must also eat their livers raw."

"Why raw and not cooked, Honorable One?"

"Because your baby girl needs the raw nourishment that only a fresh liver can provide. And, once she requires your milk no more, feed her such foods. They will help her immensely."

Days later, perhaps reflecting the rhythms of nature, the old priestess breathed her last, but not before gifting all of her worldly possessions to the young mother. Tearful, Rovena buried the ancient priestess beneath a cairn of stones in their long-favored meeting place in the forest—the one next to the mountain stream full of speckled fish.

From that day forward, mother and child lived in Hermonia's hut, a structure built with a sturdy field stone foundation, earthen bricks, and roofed over in many layers of densely woven broad-leaf boughs. Situated in the forest beneath the gnarled trunks of tall trees of great age, the mushroom-shaped structure made for a dry and warm place that was filled with Hermonia's personal treasures, gathered over a lifetime. One such treasure the old priestess bequeathed specifically to the baby girl Astra—an amulet precious beyond price, made of silver. While far too heavy for the babe to grasp much less effectively wield, Hermonia had instructed Rovena on its purpose and to hang the short-bladed knife and sheath around tiny Astra's neck at all times to protect her from evil. From that time forward, the babe and amulet become inseparable.

CHAPTER 2

The babe Astra matured as quickly as she had in the womb. By the age of four seasons, the lanky child grew strong and swift. With the gold-flecked gray eyes of her mother and black hair of her father, she bounded silently through the forest like a young deer. Early on, Rovena taught her young one all the tricks—magical and otherwise, that the witch Hermonia had taught her, and most importantly, how to use the amuletic knife and when.

By Astra's fifth season, the young girl knew how to hide and defend herself. While not quite feral, Astra grew up only knowing her mother. As for the forest, the young dhampirica was made aware that there were things in this world that were quite frightening—things like foxes, wolves, and bears.

While gathering mushrooms with her mother in the forest, an old and weakened vampire came upon the child, instinctively knowing what it represented to its like. The predator stalked from concealment, eager to reinvigorate its malnourished constitution. The crone badly muddled her approach.

The young one first caught wind of its putrid scent. Slowly, the girl dropped to one knee, pretending to examine the mossy soil, while priming her legs to spring. She glanced about with eyes only. Seeing that her mother was nowhere in sight, Astra realized she had to face this threat on her own—a threat that she had never before encountered.

She paused to take a deep breath to settle her concentration upon the rancid-smelling threat from behind. Remembering her mother's lessons, the young girl gripped her silver amulet, slowly drew its short, sharp blade, and waited for the right moment.

With eyes closed, she allowed her sensitive ears to locate the predator. *There it is! I can feel its step. It's not an animal. It's something else—not of the forest—yet only steps away!*

The young girl felt the subtle quiver of a silent footfall through her knee. *It's hovering over me ... its smell is awful!*

Now Astra! Now!

Astra turned and sprang to face her threat. Repelled by its horrific smile and rank reek of death, the child lashed out as her mother had taught her. Viciously, the stubby little blade of her silver knife—the thing gifted at birth by the good witch Hermonia—had found its mark. Only one backhanded slash was needed to seriously wound the careless hag. With its arms extended ready to pounce, Astra's three-inch silver blade had passed between them, biting deeply across the vampire's roped and leathery neck, severing much, in a splash of reeking blood. The gruesome act caused the old vampire much gurgling and gasping.

The old predator staggered back from Astra's defense while gripping her wounded neck, coughing up blood and gore. Its mouth opened and closed like a gasping fish. Its eyes flashed with a mixture of exquisite pain and absolute shock.

At that moment, Rovena appeared behind the wretch. Without a thought, she pole-axed the side of the old crone's head with a loud crack from a full swing of her staff. Now down, the old vampire sagged in an ever-widening pool of its own blood. Rovena's blow had crushed the side of its head.

Astra's initial slash, however, had covered her with the vampire's blood. Horrified, the young girl ran off to the nearby stream and jumped in, clothes and all, to cleanse herself of all trace of the evil one's putrefying scent. Once purified in the spring's ice cold waters, she returned to the kill spot and her mother.

Rovena instantly clutched her to her breast, "Are you hurt?"

"No mother."

"Look down, my love. You did well."

"Yes mother."

The pair took in the dead wretch's fallen form, which had already begun to collapse in upon itself by half. Right before their eyes, bones began to appear as its flesh visibly deteriorated. Like blackened dust motes or fluffy ash-like wisps, the vampire's flesh was carried away with each passing breath of breeze.

"By the *gods*!" Rovena whispered.

"What was that, mother?"

"I do not know my love, certainly something awful, something that cannot bear the touch of silver. Today, you did well with your blade."

"I did as you taught me," the now shivering girl said in the cradle of her mother's arms. "But what dies like that mother? *Smells* like that?"

"My love, do you remember all my stories about the most Honorable One, Hermonia?" Rovena said while caressing Astra's hair in a calming way.

"Yes mother, I do, and they were all good stories."

"It is time for another story. This one is about *things* like what we just found. It is a bad story. But before I tell it, one thing is certain. We have overstayed our presence in this valley. It is time for us to move on."

*   *   *

Within the hour, having gathered only their essential belongings and foodstuffs, the pair sadly abandoned the warm familiarity of Hermonia's abode and made way toward the valley's eastern mountain pass. During their exodus, mother and daughter traveled with extreme care so as not to leave any trace of their passage.

It was good that they had. The old vampire's sudden demise had psychically alerted the local coven, which reacted poorly to it, as the crone had been one of its elder members. Hours later, they found the old vampire's boney remains, gathered them up with reverence, and followed the perpetrator's careless footsteps back to Hermonia's earthen house. Finding it empty, and without their quarry, the coven's band torched the structure in rage.

Meanwhile, Rovena and Astra fled their home valley and continued on and on, ever fearful of the worst—pursuers. Their suspicion was confirmed when from the rocky heights they saw a smoky telltale coming from the direction of Hermonia's house.

"Did we not remember to put out the hearth?" Astra asked.

"No, we did not my love. I fear someone has set Hermonia's home afire."

"Who would do that? It was such a finely-built home, so warm and comfortable."

"Fire, my love, is the first act of mindless rage. I suspect the monster that attacked you had friends. It is good that we left in such haste."

* * *

Mother and child, now convinced of their pursuers' existence, redoubled their efforts and continued traveling east, far into the snow-topped mountains. Eventually, they descended into the green valleys of what is now northern Italy. Tired from their journey, and with their portable foodstuffs exhausted, they lived off the newfound land, which they discovered was teeming with game and enjoyed abundant streams. While Rovena snared two rabbits, Astra garnered four fish. At that evening's fire, delicious smells wafted forth upon the breeze. Their thirst sated with cold and crystalline stream water and their stomachs filled on roasted hare, spotted fish, and fresh livers for Astra, the two collapsed in each other's arms and soon began to gently snore. All was at peace.

* * *

It sniffed the air and caught the distinctive smell of a

cooking fire. With no villages about, it turned in a circle and the direction of the source was quickly surmised. Ravenous, it began to run towards it. As it neared, other scents reached its nostrils, strangely, ones that it recalled. Intrigued, it broke into an all-out sprint.

*   *   *

Rovena suddenly awoke in pain because she was being lifted to her feet by her hair. Struggling and screaming, she scratched at the powerful hand and arm that supported her.

Her captor scented the air.

"Well, well, it's the farm maid."

"You!"

But Sigmund was now looking with interest at Astra, who had crouched over to one side. She was in a low fighting stance—her knife out and at the ready.

"Don't you dare, you monster!" Rovena shrieked in terror. Her struggles renewed with a frenzied tempo as Sigmund continued to hold her firmly at arm's length.

With a reproving shake of the head Sigmund said, "I warned you, fair farm maid. Now I will collect what is mine."

With a quick twist of Rovena's hair, the woman's

neck twisted grotesquely right to expose her neck. With preternatural speed, Sigmund fell to one knee, laid Rovena's back across it, and bit deeply into her neck. The woman's reaction was electric. Her spine arched as she desperately kicked and scratched at anything within reach. Then, Rovena sagged in total submission.

At this point Astra saw her chance and attacked. While the monster was bent over her mother, the young girl flew through the air with her knife held aloft in both hands. Landing on Sigmund's back, Astra plunged her knife into his thickly muscled shoulder once, twice … creating deep, ragged wounds that freely bled. In response, the monster flicked her off like a fly. Landing awkwardly some ten feet away, Astra managed to roll back into a defensive fighting stance.

Pausing with blood dripping from his mouth, "So the little one is a fighter too! How *refreshing*," Sigmund roared at her. "Just like this delicious farm maid."

Then, he suddenly went still, smacking his lips, and sniffed the air once again toward the girl-child as if to confirm something. "No, the farm maid … is your mother … and that makes you … my … daughter!" the vampire roared. "Your smell is of my loins!"

"No!" Astra screamed back in horrified defiance. The cords of her neck strained with effort as she again flew through the air at her mother's attacker. She slashed wildly at the vampire's face, just nicking his right cheek as he batted her away again.

Sigmund laughed in her face. "Yes, little one, you are indeed my daughter. You have my vicious spirit. And in time, you will join my kind, just as your mother will."

"No, never!"

"So you say!" Sigmund smiled wickedly. "I will leave your mother to finish you. I have taken my fill." The monster carelessly allowed Rovena's limp form to roll off his knee onto the ground as he stood up.

He slowly backed up beyond the firelight and disappeared into the night, leaving behind his bloody carnage.

*　　*　　*

Astra did not move for several moments as she remained primed to defend herself. Twice she thought she heard a footfall. But eventually, she crawled over to her mother's moaning fallen body, whose chest rose and fell with short, raspy breaths. At taking in her plight, Astra gasped out, "Oh, mother!"

"My love …" came the weak, gurgling reply.

When Astra turned her mother's head to reveal the

mortal wound, she gagged at its sight.

"My love … use your knife … press its silver blade against my wounds … please … it will stop the bleeding … and maybe more …"

Astra did as her mother asked, but it was not easy. Whenever the blade came into contact with her mother's' wounds, the skin sizzled and burned, while Rovena groaned and writhed.

"Do not stop, my love. You are saving me!"

Finally finished with her grim work, the left side of Rovena's neck had become a bruised blue-black, and seared mass. But the profuse bleeding had stopped.

"My love … gather wood for a fire. And … sufficient green vines for two stout rabbit snares."

Without thinking, Astra answered, "Yes, mother, I will."

It took three trips in all, but Astra soon had rekindled the fire into a roaring blaze that lit up the surrounding forest. The two women huddled in its warmth.

"We must sleep," Rovena whispered. "But before we do, tightly bind my wrists and ankles with the rabbit snares."

"What?"

"My love … do as you are told … please."

After Astra did so, Rovena smiled, "Such a fine daughter you are. Now I will sleep on this side of the fire … you the other."

*   *   *

That was the last time I saw my mother. Sometime in the night she had somehow broken the green vines that I had so firmly bound her with. Their frayed fragments lay on the ground next to the fire's circle, their knots intact.

Then I remembered the monster's parting words: "In time, you will join my kind, just as your mother will." The connection was made. My cowardly father had left me with my poisoned mother to eventually poison me with his wickedness. This fact my mother must have understood, and yet refused to give into. She had left me that night to protect me yet again, but this time, from her.

CHAPTER 3

As I look back on my seventh season, I had become a truly wild child of the forest, who actively sought out monsters—all the while hoping to find and slay my father. As I roamed from place to place, I discovered that the countryside was rife with them. That season alone, I hunted down and killed five such smelly things. While none were my father—or my mother for that matter, their scent betrayed that he had poisoned them with his evil.

In all ways, I lived at a different level of existence than mortals. They went about their lives locked in a never-ending cycle of pursing pleasure and avoiding pain. I saw and experienced things otherwise. Pain was a reliable, strict, and absolute teacher incapable of treachery. It was there for a reason—be it an injury, an encounter with a dangerous animal, or delivered as a frightened child's glance filled with horror and rejection that stung deeply in the heart.

Life was harsh in those days, despite the plentiful game and fish. I was living at the margins of two worlds: one of monsters and the other of mortal kind. Both situations were devoid of any detectable semblance of civility. Immersed in that environment, my innate senses developed at a terrific rate. Now with grim purpose, they quickly tuned far beyond the mortal norm. As for my own scent—something that even my mother's concealment spell could not mask, I masked it by bathing daily in cold streams and sleeping in pine boughs.

Now a creature of the forests and glens, I developed a crafty hunter's intuition along with a distinct lust to kill monsters. But down deep, I blamed my situation on my monster father who I never really knew, yet, who had influenced my existence so very much.

This easily explained the lightness of my sleep, as I always and everywhere unconsciously looked over my shoulder, expecting to see my father's lurid grin. I yearned to confront him, to kill him, or be taken in the act. I truly did not care. All I wanted was to be able to once again sleep a deep sleep.

During this time, I wandered widely, avoided making any acquaintances, and while doing so stumbled upon a gruesome side to my existence. I discovered I had a marked preference for the blood-engorged fresh livers of the wild game that I caught. Eating such internal parts warmed my skin and tangibly increased my strength and endurance.

I must admit that this preference my mother had impressed upon me, for early on, she had fed me such fresh livers. Then, while preparing a fresh deer kill, my taste for bloody, uncooked meats now came to the fore. I could not stop licking my fingers. With every morsel my dhampiric side rejoiced, but hungered for more, ever more. Only later would I realize that this nourishment had extended my life span greatly.

By the end of my seventh season, my predations upon the region's local monsters had earned me a reputation as a protectoress of children and the aged—after having saved both. This I learned from concealment, while overhearing their thankful entreaties and prayers for my behalf. At the same time, the local covens who shielded these monsters and counted them within their membership had taken note. On two occasions, they sent out their own huntsmen, who in turn became my prey. No, I did not eat their livers, but the thought *had* crossed my mind.

Early on in my eighth season word of my presence had eventually reached the ears of a middle-aged Etruscan priestess named Lethi. This kind soul, devoted to the Etruscan goddess Vecu—the guardian of graves, sought me out. Only now do I fully appreciate what a risk she had taken in doing so.

Much like my mother Rovena, who had been befriended by the aged witch Hormonia, Lethi adopted me outright into her temple community within the Etruscan walled city of Velathri. Within the walls of the temple, which at first I found stifling and claustrophobic, Lethi patiently began the process of transforming me into a civilized being. Without question, this was a hard time for me, full of misunderstandings, outright mistakes, thievery, remorse, and self-discovery. But because of Lethi's many kindnesses, I found that I could sleep deeply through the night.

During my initial days at the temple, I was told just what my father was. Yes, he was a monster, but a monster with a specific name—*vrykólakas* in the Greek tongue. But far more importantly, they found out what I was—a *dhampirica*.

In the fullness of time, I learned to care for myself, read and write, and above all, to socialize with the rest of the temple community. That in itself was quite a challenge for this wild forest imp. Along the way I learned that the Etruscan priestesses of Vecu guarded the cemeteries, despised grave robbers, and fought against vampires and any other *things* that might threaten the sanctity of the *necropoleis*. Here, all of my natural abilities and hunting skills found their place, and as a result, became honed further to a knife-edge. During my twelfth year, I twice intercepted *things* that attempted to break into a grave. I learned that such creatures did not wander about alone, but instead gathered within the sanctuary of covens—especially those in that accursed city of oppression—Rome, where, I was told, far too many were granted safe harbor.

Time for me passed all too quickly. I matured, came to enjoy the temple's peace and solitude, and naturally took my guard duties at the *necropoleis* seriously. When I outlived my patroness Lethi, who passed at the age of sixty-three seasons, I rightfully took her place within the order.

Upon reflection, my time within the Temple of Vecu coincided with a remarkable tranquility within the many *necropoleis*, which remained largely unmolested. In fact, the entire region and its walled city enjoyed a vampire-free existence. The local coven waned. Was that entirely because of me? Not entirely, but I did offer assistance when asked.

Once a child, now a woman, I possessed an amazing longevity because of my taste for fresh livers. During my second century within the order, I became its high priestess. By the second century AD, despite my best efforts at recruitment, the temple of Vecu spiraled into decline. Why? Because our order had performed our duties all too well. On the one hand, there were no *dhampir* to recruit, because their vampiric source had been removed. More troubling, the local population had forgotten what the scourge of vampirism had been like. Instead they were now enchanted by the glittering novelty of imported pagan deities from exotic lands. And then there was the eternal promise made by Christianity.

Above all, throughout years I, Astra, hunter of monsters, still anticipated an eventual encounter with my father. I knew in my heart that he was out there—somewhere. This reality I accepted. How? I cannot say. Just that I was as sure of its truth as the next rising of the sun.

Still, despite all of my hunting experience and temple training, I had doubts. When the time came, I did not know whether I could kill my father, or whether Sigmund would kill me. Nonetheless, I stand ready with my birthright—Hermonia's silver knife. Perhaps when that inevitable time comes, I will possess the resolve to strike swiftly and with deadly purpose.

CHAPTER 4

Tall, well-muscled, dark-haired with long curls, and with golden skin, the vampire journeyed widely, embracing opportunistically the old, sick, young, drunken, and foolish, before moving on. Occasionally, after an inadvertent indiscretion, a local populace would realize his presence. In response, they predictably rose up and shooed him away like a pestilential insect.

Sigmund had indeed spent considerable time in northern Italy, but had purposely avoided the territories controlled by the Etruscan walled cities. Their defenses, both architectural and religious, had a reputation decidedly caustic to his kind.

The times had become dangerous. Rumors of his passing spread like the wind from village to village along the Roman roads. Vexed by this development, Sigmund decided to end his endless wanderings and instead hide anonymously within many. Sigmund chose to do what was natural for any predator—he traveled south in search of richer hunting grounds. In this case that meant the city of Rome, a place of immense power, wealth, and shocking poverty. There, so went the rumor, one of his kind could "hide" among its vast urban mob and plunder it at will.

To his delight, he discovered further safeguards within that city's vast walls, as Rome possessed a large, well-organized, and ancient coven. This enclave traced its roots back to Egyptian Memphis, and before that, the Mesopotamian city of Ur. For the mere sum of two silver sesterces, Sigmund eagerly joined its membership. Now he was not alone, for *others* had made the same calculation. These *others* were much like he, but of many different kinds. Collectively, they called themselves the Hidden Folk, who organized their kind within the ancient coven.

The *Consilium magorum et sagarum*, the "Council of Magicians and Witches," privately met on a regular basis within a patrician villa located just north of Rome. Below it, a useful warren of catacomb-like tunnels and rooms were under construction by those in debt to the villa's owner. Most, if not all of these unfortunates, never would ever again see the light of day. Instead, their remains became part of these vast underground works.

The *Consilium*, like all such organizations, had long established rules of decorum, ceremonies, initiations, meetings, and elders. Such things were new to Sigmund, an old predator long set in his solitary ways.

But the relative new-comer, long used to the wide-open freedoms of a rural setting, soon found himself breaking the coven's rules far too often. To ensure the coven's existence and security under the Roman eagle, its membership had to adhere to several strict and basic tenets. Since human sacrifice was deemed abhorrent by Roman law, therefore, all such activities and their traces were strictly overseen by the coven and were sanctioned only for important religious "feast" days. As for those members who depended upon human flesh for their very existence, draconian "rules" of discretion and delicacy reigned supreme and were not to be broached. While these rules of engagement had been explained to the vampire, he nevertheless could not grasp the need for such prohibitions.

Soon the vampire's unbridled plunder of the Roman mob threatened the coven's very existence. They raised a vociferous clamor and made noisy complaints upon the Roman authorities demanding protection and swift action. Clearly, they argued, some kind of beast was stalking Rome's streets and alleys. They were correct.

Since Roman statute law explicitly prohibited homicide, investigations into the grisly murders ensued. The vampire's flagrant disregard for the *Consilium*'s tenets, regarding the taking of human victims within Rome's walls, had quickly became unacceptable, as the predator typically left its bloodless victims in the city's streets and byways. Such unwanted notice that *things* lived within Rome's walls the *Consilium* knew the mob, Senate, and emperor would not tolerate. To the vampire Sigmund, he was oblivious to the public outcry and only saw a vast sea of blood, ripe for the taking.

After two particularly outrageous instances—both of well-known matrons, word finally reached the floor of the Imperial Senate that something must be done about this threat to the public safety. The emperor at that time, Caracallus, had in the previous year extended Roman citizenship to all free inhabitants of the empire. Many within the Senate found this development repugnant, believing that their highly-prized status had been grossly degraded. Rumors said the newly-made citizens often brought with them an evil plague of some sort. The whispers even suggested that perhaps the emperor somehow had a hand in this—all to threaten the welfare of the long-established Roman nobility.

Pressured by that august body, the emperor personally promised swift action. He dispatched the Praetorian Guard to round up some suspects. Among them, and by sheer chance, were collected several

Hidden Folk of the *Consilium*, who under examination, sang like starlings. Shocked by what they were hearing and feeling out of their depth, their inquisitors deferred to the emperor himself, who held the title chief high priest of Rome—the *pontifex maximus*. He would make the judgment.

To ensure the secrecy of the highly-charged testimony, Caracallus ordered the quiet execution of the suspects, and then exacted sworn oaths of secrecy from his inquisitors, who he then poisoned. The emperor would not tolerate a faction called the *Consilium* existing within Rome's walls. He wanted them rooted out. His faithful Praetorians would be his instrument.

As the Roman authorities began to close their net around the coven, its leadership had few choices. Somehow, some way, they needed to immediately redirect the administration's interest while they internally silenced the troublemaker.

Through a clever deception, the *Consilium* diverted the emperor's ire by providing damning evidence in the form of a letter about the activities and practices of a suitable sacrificial goat—the Christians. So was laid the root cause for the historical enmity between the Roman Church and the *Consilium magorum et sagarum*, known today as simply CMES.

With the Roman mob, Senate, and emperor so placated, the leadership of the *Consilium* breathed a sigh of relief, before it looked inward to address the source of their unwanted exposure. A council was summoned to decide how best to deal with one of its own. Unanimously, the council dispatched forty *iudices magicae*, or "judges of magic," who were charged with the capture and dispatch of the vampire Sigmund for his repeated and blatant "excesses."

CHAPTER 5

The furious chase of the vampire Sigmund led the *Consilium*'s forty judges along the entire length of Italy. Hurrying south along the paved road system of the empire, Sigmund planned to lose his pursuers at the busy port city of Brindisium, located at the heel of the Apennine Peninsula. Meanwhile, the judges countered that ploy with the use of enchanted pigeons, which carried messages about the fugitive, his description, and what to do if seen, to their brethren located throughout the peninsula.

Sigmund's hurried passage south was soon reported, but in many ways, was merely a confirmation. For before the vampire reached that harbor city, Sigmund had left behind a bloody trail. He garishly dispatched four of the judges while en route—vampires all—who had foolishly run ahead of the others. Their mad blood lust was to put an end to one of their own, restore some semblance of their clannish pride, and so rid their coven of this blemish. They failed miserably, as their wily prey had ambushed each and every one of them. Before the last expired, Sigmund extracted from it who and how many pursued him. Armed with that knowledge, the vampire set more ambushes, watched for the flight of pigeons, while redoubling his speed toward Brindisium.

Once there, Sigmund planned on catching the first departing boat and disappearing into the provinces of the vast eastern Roman Empire. As luck would have it, he boarded a small trading vessel headed for Illyricum, a destination just opposite Brindisium on the other side of the Adriatic Sea. Lumbering and slow, the passage of the sailing ship took three days instead of the usual one or two. That decision made in haste would come to haunt the fleeing vampire.

Upon reaching the Illyrian harbor town of Dyrrachium, the remaining judges, who had hired an oared sailing ship, captured the vampire as he disembarked on the wharf. Originally forty in number, their pursuit of the vampire and his many ambushes had cost their band dearly. Twelve fell in the mad dash across Italy alone, another eight on the Dyrrachian wharf. With their numbers halved, they finally subdued the demon, ensnaring Sigmund within a heavy fisherman's net. Weighed down and trapped within its soggy mass, the judges rolled him up within it like a weaver's rug and loaded the whole upon a hired livery cart. The leader, Lucius Appius and *pontifex* of the Egyptian god Set, purchased masonry hammers, rope, and iron spikes mounted with rings in the port. These items, and others deemed needful, were deposited in the cart along with their captive.

Through the good graces of the local Dyrrachium coven, which was more than happy to assist their Roman brethren, the remaining judges were told of an appropriate location to secretly execute their final judgment. After a half day's travel, the weary band arrived with their prize at a forest clearing in the nearby mountains, which was dominated by a prominent mound covered with a long, luxuriant, green grass.

"Here men," said Lucius Appius, "is where we will dispose of this vile creature. But first we must find the tomb's entrance. I examine its eastern side carefully."

In no time, the tomb's low arched entrance was laid bare. Made of dressed limestone blocks, the tomb's obvious age caused grumbling comments by several.

"Lucius," one asked, "will we be cursed for defiling this sacred place?"

After some thought, "Probably not Atticus, for our need is far greater. Our cause is just. We are dispatching a monster from this realm."

Levers were then brought to bear and the tomb's sealing blocks quickly breached, causing much dust and foul air to escape.

"Such great treasure," murmured one upon entering the mound, "and such fine weaponry! This is the burial of a prince, or perhaps, a king!" His ever-rising avaricious voice echoed oddly within the domed chamber.

Shouldering his way past the greedy one into the cramped space, Lucius Appius tersely ordered with dark eyes flashing, "Brush it all aside. Make way for a broad, clear area in the center." And after another moment, "And not one thing is to be taken from this burial. Not one!" he emphasized with an upraised finger. "I will not have any plunder taken from such a noble individual," he finished with a stern look. "Further, I do not know which god protects this place. What we are about to do just might disturb it."

Five men entered the cleared center with the heavy hammers and iron stakes with wharf rings. They began to pound these iron additions into the tomb's bedrock flooring, forming a rough pentagram wide enough to stretch a man.

*   *   *

During these preparations, the vampire Sigmund silently looked on from his place on the cart amid the netting. From there he observed, marshaled his strength, and waited for any opportunity to break free. Sigmund knew that trussed up as he was, at some point the netting had to be cut away. Then would be his best chance. Since he had already killed the four swift vampires of this lynch mob, he knew that no one else among the remaining rabble was fast enough to run him down.

*   *   *

Once in place, the men strung thick ropes through the five iron rings that ended in stout silver manacles. The trick, Lucius Appius knew, was getting those bonds on his victim.

He strode over to the ladened down cart, and said, "Sigmund. I have an offer to make."

"Speak Egyptian."

"You are a brave vampire. You have fought bravely during our pursuit. I have already lost many judges, and I do not wish to lose any more. If you do not resist during your shackling, I promise a swift, clean death. What is your answer?"

"As I am not yet so restrained, and as Egyptians are renowned for their clever riddles and promises, what is your guarantee?"

"My word, vampire."

Sigmund's answer flew through the air. The spittle landed squarely on the priest of Set's carefully painted face, who did not attempt to remove it. "I will remember this insult vampire. And I can assure you, that you will as well. By the way, I am immune to your evil ways."

And so the preparations began. Once they rolled the mass of netting from the cart, Lucius sent three of his men off with the cart on an errand. With the remaining seventeen, which included himself, they brought out the four silver shackles and their attending ropes from the tomb.

"Men, we will fight this monster to the end. Show no mercy. Grant no reprieve. We have grim work ahead of us. We will bind him one wrist at a time, one ankle at a time. And then, we will pull him into the tomb, and stretch him like a sail between the rings. Let us begin."

Many knives began cutting away at the netting. As they did so, Sigmund gathered himself within his robes into a tight ball. This Lucius suspected he would do. The Egyptian *pontifex* also knew that there was a very good chance he would lose several more judges before the vampire was firmly trussed up in the tomb. It would be grim work indeed.

* * *

The slow and methodical nature of the Egyptian priest's preparations troubled Sigmund. He orchestrated his minions precisely, calmly, with the assurance of someone who had preformed this task before. It caused a shiver to quake through the vampire's usually confident nature, not to mention what would become of him once they shackled him. He clearly saw the silver bonds. He knew what they would do to him. And so, at that moment, Sigmund realized that this was no longer a game, but indeed serious business. If he was to escape, he would have to marshal all of his strength and guile to do so.

*   *   *

Just as Lucius Appius had foreseen, the clamping of the first silver shackle cost him two judges. The crafty vampire had dangled his hand like bait, and before his men could react, two had lost their throats. But the price was worth it, for the rest of his men had pinned down that arm and shackled it. The vampire had screamed so loud that his agony reverberated in their chests.

Now with an arm limp of its strength and with the silver's touch wracking his brain, the deadly contest continued. Next was secured the head in a leather horse-like halter with a silver bit. Drawn harshly back, the burning metal jammed open Sigmund's mouth, preventing him from biting another judge. One unfortunate had already received a vicious mauling of his forearm. While still unconscious, Lucius Appius had ordered the judge's throat mercifully cut and head removed, as he could smell the vampire's foulness in the man. Andronicus had been a good friend. He would not leave him in such a sorry state.

Now clearly in a state of frantic panic, Sigmund fought on, crushing a judge's head with his grip. But while doing so, the second silver manacle was clamped into place, rendering his second arm useless. Yet, the struggle did not stop. In the course of binding his ankles, another judge suffered a destroyed knee from a vicious kick. Screaming in pain and understanding what must be done, Lucius Appius put him out of his misery.

Thirteen men now dragged the vampire into the tomb. Before doing so, they had plugged their ears and wrapped their heads with many layers of cloth to deaden the deafening roars and howls that they knew would reverberate off of the domed roof. With the five ropes stretched tight on the iron rings like a ship's creaking rigging, the vampire could not move. Now totally helpless and defenseless, Sigmund's robes were cut away, many knifes were honed into razors, and the truly grim work of flaying the monster alive began.

Lucius Appius organized his judges into teams of two, each instructed to fill their bucket with their carvings. The priest of Set did not offer a reason for this fastidiousness, just that one team at a time would work on the vampire until their bucket was filled. Once filled, the team was to completely burn their carvings upon the fire. So destroyed, the team gathered the ashes and dumped them into the river. Only then did Lucius Appius allow them to purify themselves and their clothing in the river. The *pontifex* of Set also made the following prohibitions: no one was to touch the vampire's head, neck, or torso—only the limbs were to be defleshed.

By day's end, the fifth team emerged with only a half-bucket filled. Seeing this, Lucius Appius grunted with approval and entered the tomb for the first time since the gruesome work began. The stench was overwhelming. The bedrock flooring was slick with blood, urine, and excrement. Once muscular limbs had been methodically reduced to bone, sinew, and not much else. The priest bent over and examined the dusty and tear-streaked face. It stared back, somehow still defiant. With a smirk of pleasure, Lucius Appius removed two silver Greek drachmas from his pocket.

"See these, vampire?" and he spat down on his face. "This is only the beginning," he said, as he bent down and placed the two coins on the monster's eyes. Immediately they began their burning descent to the bottom of their orbits. Immediately in accompaniment, the screaming renewed in long lasting, horrific howls of the damned.

When the priest of Set emerged from the tomb into the open air, he did so with a gasp of relief. Presently, the three dispatched earlier on an errand arrived with the livery cart ladened down with three large wine *amphorae*. Eying these containers, the surviving judges thought Lucius Appius had thoughtfully planned a drunken party after all their grim work. This was not the case.

"Seal up the entrance to the height of a man's waist." He tersely ordered.

When that task was completed, Lucius Appius commanded the three *amphorae* to be unloaded and brought to the partially sealed tomb. The men found that the containers were oddly light in weight and did not slosh with liquid.

"Carefully open this amphora and pour its contents into the tomb."

To the men's surprise, once the lid was removed a

din of squealing erupted on their ears. As the massive jar was lifted into position, out came a flood of mole rats, which fell, scampered, and disappeared into the dank darkness of the tomb. They represented dozens upon dozens of hungry mouths that needed to feed.

Just as the third jar was so emptied, one of the judges holding it carelessly by its rim had a finger nipped. The result was the container crashed to the ground and shattered.

"Marcus, that was clumsy," Lucius Appius observed as several of the mole rats escaped going this way and that. "If I did not know better, I would have thought that you favored the vampire in some way."

Holding his bleeding finger tightly to his chest, "I am sorry, Honorable One. It will not happen again."

"Indeed," the priest said, as he unsheathed his ritual dagger and slit the man's throat. "Judges, help this one into the tomb."

Struggling while still holding his throat, many hands quickly overcame him and in over the low wall he went.

Only then was the tomb's entrance finally sealed. As Lucius Appius ritualistically placed the last block in position, he heard a muffled whimper from within, from whom he did not care.

However, one last task remained. The priest of Set cast a curse over the grassy mound that was more lasting than the salting of its earth. "In three days time, none shall thrive or spawn at this place."

Once this awful spell triggered, it denied all life, and transformed the burial mound into a barren hillock incongruously surrounded by a lush mountain forest.

The year was AD 215.

PART II: PRESENT DAY

CHAPTER 1

Near a small village on the western slopes of Mount Dajti, Albania, many hands carefully restored a late Roman mountain fortification. The government funded, university-lead project required that local labor be employed. Early on in the restoration, an elderly local woman named Ajola found a part-time job as the project's cook. A happy grandmother, she marvelously fit the bill.

Gjyshe Ajola, "Grandma Ajola," was much loved by the archaeological staff and local laborers for her homey hot meals, effervescent personality, and powerfully brewed aromatic teas. She always made sure that everyone left her tables full and satisfied. It was not uncommon for her to stuff an apple into someone's pocket. As a consequence, anything that disturbed the daily mood and gastronomic harmony of his restoration effort, the archaeological director had to address.

But Ajola was special in other ways. Her dreams were often clairvoyant and she had a knack for mending children's broken bones and healing their fevers. This made *Gjyshe* Ajola well-known throughout the district, and while she did not know it, the grandmother was a Class A sensitive and healer. In another time, another place, *Gjyshe* Ajola would have been a much-revered priestess or witch.

Professor Dr. L. Galaty nervously rubbed his bearded chin when he heard the cook's story. Despite his long and rigorous formal university education, his upbringing nonetheless carried with it a fair dose of folklore and superstition. The cook, a round and short figure, who usually wore a perpetual smile, had experienced something on her way to the restoration site's kitchen that his own grandmother had once confided to him. Namely, that some places were cursed and some individuals could feel the power of that evil. Now with graying streaks in his hair, his grandmother's stories returned to him as he listened to the cook's tale.

"So, *Gjyshe* Ajola, tell me about what happened yesterday morning during your walk to base camp," the archaeological director began, noting the woman's dark circles around dull, sleepless eyes. She looked down, fidgeted, and seemed uncomfortable. This was not his *gjyshe*.

"*Profesor* Galaty, I walk to the camp's kitchen from the mountain tram station every morning for my health. The exercise keeps me young. It is my way," the sixty-something said as she cocked her head and tried a perky smile, but failed. "I always wish to find new ways to walk. I like to explore. I like variety, I suppose," she said with a shrug. "So yesterday I took a different way through the woods. I found an overgrown path that looked promising. After some meters, it became an old paved road—much like the ones you are studying. I was intrigued, so I followed it. The road led to a clearing in the forest and passed through it by going around a small hill in its center. But *Profesor* Galaty, nothing, absolutely nothing grew in that clearing or on that small hill. Yet, all around," she gestured in amazement with her hands, "the forest is everywhere lush and green," she finished, while unnecessarily examining her heavy hands.

"So what troubled you, *Gjyshe* Ajola?"

Again the old woman fidgeted before speaking. "*Profesor* Galaty, you are a good and educated man. I never went to school. I barely read and write," she said with a shrug and open palms. "I don't know how to say this, but when I entered that clearing a great weight pressed down on me. My heart felt as if a great hand squeezed it. I almost fell sick. As I rounded the small hill on the stone path, I knew, *Profesor* Galaty, this feeling of, of dread and horror came from it, the hill. *Profesor* Galaty, that little hill is full of evil. It contains a *horrible* secret. I can feel it in my bones, *profesor*."

Several moments passed between the two as Galaty gathered his composure following her highly-charged and emotional revelation.

"Did this path lead out of the clearing, *Gjyshe* Ajola, and back into the forest?"

Much relieved, "Yes, *Profesor* Galaty, yes it did! And that evil feeling went away once I reentered the forest."

"Are you willing to show me this place, *Gjyshe* Ajola?"

Again the elderly woman avoided his eyes and answered without looking up, "I do not wish to."

"If I showed you a map, do you think that you could show me where this place is?"

Now brightening noticeably, "I would be happy to try, *Profesor* Galaty!"

"Good. We will talk again after lunch."

*   *   *

Later that morning the archaeological director thought he knew every nook and cranny of the mountainous region under his jurisdiction, but after consulting Google Earth, a conspicuous bare spot, with a small mound, stuck out like a sore thumb on his laptop's screen. Even the traces of a paved road could be seen.

"Now how did I miss that?" he said under his breath and to no one in particular.

As he scanned in and out, he squinted at the image and pinched his lower lip in thought. *Might this be an Illyrian burial mound?*

* * *

Later that day, a Tuesday, Ajola vowed to tell her priest about her dreadful experience. She had to get it off her chest. So she went to the evening Novena services at her parish church, the Church of the Sacred Heart, in Tirana. Before the service, Ajola made her confession and poured out her troubled soul to her priest. She told him of her visions of agony, blood, and pain. Of a band of evil men who tortured another to death. The middle-aged Father Jetmir was not shocked by what the elderly matron described, for she was well-known within his parish as the local sensitive. Just last spring during another such confession, she had correctly confided to the priest the identity of a man she had seen in a vision, who had brutally murdered a young woman.

Once the Novena services concluded, Father Jetmir paid a visit to his superior, the archbishop.

"Your Eminence, thank you for receiving me at such a late hour."

"Nonsense, Father Jetmir," the stooped white-haired cleric smiled from behind his sparse wooden desk. With his hands folded before him, "I take it that what you bring me at this hour cannot be good news."

"Sadly, you are correct, Your Eminence. I have just heard something that the Vatican might want to look into."

"Not the local authorities, as before with the murder of that poor young soul?"

"No, Your Eminence. I believe this issue is quite outside the jurisdiction of our local authorities."

"I see, Father Jetmir. Please then, tell me all about it."

The next day, Cardinal Alberti in Rome read the Albanian archbishop's account on his laptop with considerable interest. The reason why the good cardinal received the archbishop's email was because he was the operations director of Pro Deo—the Vatican's paranormal research department.

CHAPTER 2

Professor Dr. Erik Gerhardt Reissen was thoroughly enjoying his second career as a paranormal archaeologist. Employed by the Vatican, actually a member of its Pro Deo department, Reissen kept current on his former egyptological career, while he explored the limits of his psychic side.

Because of his Vatican training, the Austrian now saw his former studies in ancient Egyptian magic through a fresh set of eyes. He noted the ancient Egyptian's use of select vocabulary, and their actions performed with a broader appreciation. He better appreciated the limitations of the Egyptian language, and how the magicians of the time had stretched the boundaries of their psychic reality within the constraints of their language. Reissen realized his ancient counterparts had developed a magical code heavily dosed with metaphorical language.

Reissen's daily regime meant that he was up early for a morning run through the ancient city's streets. Following a shower at his flat, he stopped for a breakfast espresso and sweet, followed by a brisk walk to his office at the Gregorian Museum. Life was good.

On this day unfortunately, he had granted 3Sat, an

Austrian TV channel, a follow-up interview on his excavation of the Egyptian magician Djedi's tomb.

As preparations for the telecast were taking place and the bright camera lighting positioned, Reissen was casually-seated before one of his overflowing bookcases. Tan, chisel-jawed, lean, and with shock black hair swept back by the station's stylist covering his ears, the woman behind the camera saw him as a natural movie star. To enhance that image, she softened her otherwise harsh portrait lens ever so slightly.

In the midst of the usual barrage of questions, Reissen recognized he had become Austria's modern-day answer to Britain's Howard Carter. He allowed himself to relax and enjoy the moment, but remained careful not to slip up on the heavily paranormal aspects of that excavation, all of which were embargoed by his Vatican masters. Then, perhaps sensing the archaeologist's guard had dropped, the interviewer sprung an unexpected question.

"Professor Reissen, following your highly-successful excavation of the Djedi tomb, have you been back to Egypt?"

Reissen blinked back as the interviewer, a charming, green-eyed woman with gleaming white teeth, had caught him completely flat-footed.

"Well … ah … yes … I was asked to inspect an ancient monument by Egypt's Supreme Council of Antiquities."

The woman, sensing his reticence, quickly followed up, "Can you tell our audience about it?"

Reissen theatrically paused. "Not really. In fact, do you remember the story about an explosion in the Egyptian Western Desert near Sakkara?"

With widening eyes, "Why yes, yes I do."

"Well, a natural gas pocket caused that explosion. When it blew, it ruined a Fourth Dynasty structure in the vicinity. To this day, we do not know what that structure's function was, as it was entirely destroyed," Reissen smoothly lied into the red-eyed lens with all the conviction he could muster.

*   *   *

Four weeks later, and after the Austrian telecast of his interview, Reissen received a call from his former departmental chairman, Professor Dr. Gustav Höhenfelder, of the University of Vienna.

"Erik, this is Höhenfelder. I watched your interview last night on 3Sat. You look marvelous!"

"Thank you, Gustav. How very kind of you to call," Reissen skated uneasily as he already knew where this conversation would ultimately lead.

After an awkward silence, Höhenfelder got down to business.

"Erik. How can I ask this? You are currently on a much-deserved sabbatical following the Djedi project, but I have not received any indication if you intend to return to the department. May I ask, do your future plans include the university?"

With a heavy heart, Reissen heard himself say, "I am very sorry, Gustav, I deeply apologize for not writing my intentions sooner, but I will not be returning to the university. My research here at the Vatican has become all consuming. Again, I apologize for not having informed you earlier."

"I see," Höhenfelder said with a small voice tinged with genuine regret. "We will miss you Erik. And privately, if your situation ever changes, please do not hesitate to call me."

"Thank you Gustav. Your many kindnesses over the years will not be forgotten."

*　　*　　*

After that call from Höhenfelder, Reissen realized perhaps for the first time, just how committed he was to his new career and his own psychic development.

While he had just burned a significant bridge something that he seldom, if ever, did, he felt relieved that he had done it. As he was thinking about this watershed moment in his career, his office phone buzzed again jarring him from his thoughts.

"*Ciao*, Dr. Reissen, this is Cardinal Alberti's office. His Eminence would like to see you today. Are you available?"

"Absolutely. I can be there in ten minutes if needed."

"Superb. I will inform the cardinal. He will be waiting for you."

First Höhenfelder and now my new Vatican superior Alberti, and on the same day. I must be a popular fellow.

During the brief walk from Reissen's office to the cardinal's administrative suite, Reissen could not help but wonder if the good cleric had another assignment for him. Egypt naturally came to mind, his first love, and second home. Besides, such a visit would be an opportunity to speak Arabic, which he felt had become rusty.

The cardinal's office was fronted by a small but richly-paneled reception area with a luxurious Persian rug. The brass work on the door hinges and knobs possessed that marvelous mix of the green patina of age and shiny gleam of use. A young priest sat behind the receptionist desk.

Walking directly up to the priest, Reissen announced himself while thinking, *he's new.*

"*Al momento, Professore* Reissen, he said." head down, rapidly typing a handful of key strokes into his laptop. His index finger then stabbed the ENTER key.

Yes Erik, he's new.

Moments later, a single chime was heard and the priest gestured Reissen with an open hand towards the cardinal's office door.

"Thank you, father."

"*Prego, professore.*"

For Reissen, entering the lion's den had become a bit of a game. Resting his hand on the heavy wooden door before knocking, the archaeologist liked to reach out with his highly-attuned perception to feel out its occupant's mood. This time, he was rewarded with a tangible sense of "excitement" from the other side of door. The archaeologist took that "read" as a positive. He knocked.

"*Entrare Herr* Dr. Reissen."

As the archaeologist had closed the door behind him, Cardinal Alberti said, "Thank you for stopping by my office on such short notice, Dr. Reissen," the cleric in the red vestment said as he rose from behind his desk while extending his hand in greeting. As before, that physical contact was simply electric, as the cardinal was a powerful sensitive.

Once everyone was seated, "Dr. Reissen," Cardinal Alberti began, "I have the perfect assignment for you," the cleric declared from behind his ornate wooden office desk—a massive antique of great age—with his fingers steepled before him.

"Such as, Your Eminence? You have piqued my interest. What sort of paranormal crisis is now brewing in Egypt?"

"Always so direct. I like that. But, no, Dr. Reissen, this crisis is not in Egypt."

Reissen face fell. "Not in Egypt?"

"No, Dr. Reissen, your next deployment will be to Albania."

"Albania?"

"There is an archaeological site there—actually located in the former Roman province of Epirus Nova—that needs to be psychically assessed. In fact, we need your impressions about that site as soon as possible."

"But Your Eminence, I am a trained Egyptian

archaeologist. I know next to nothing about Balkan archaeology, chronology, or history. Why me?"

Secretly enjoying Reissen's consternation because it dented the Austrian's usually cool demeanor, the cardinal continued. "Why you? Because Dr. Reissen, you are the perfect candidate for this paranormal assessment, precisely because you harbor no preconceived biases whatsoever. Besides, it will be an enriching growth experience, and the truth is, our work does not always take us to our favorite haunts."

Now folding his hands before him, fingers interlacing, the cardinal went on. "Further, you are an experienced dirt archaeologist and field director. Those are valuable assets. The society needs your eyes in the field Dr. Reissen, not only to assess the site, but to understand the local logistics if we decide to intervene."

Now opening a manila folder on his immaculate leather desk blotter, the Roman cleric removed a large photograph and handed it over to the Austrian. "Here, Dr. Reissen. Take a look at this overhead and tell me what you see."

With the crisp, color, aerial photo in his hands, Reissen asked, "At what altitude was this shot taken?"

"Approximately one hundred meters."

A grunt, then, "Why is this mound without

vegetation? Was it recently cleared for this aerial?"

"No, Dr. Reissen. What you see is the pristine site. To our best knowledge, no one has touched it in … perhaps … centuries … or even millennia."

The Austrian whistled. "If that is indeed the case, this barrenness is a mystery. What's the rest of the terrain look like?"

In anticipation of the archaeologist's question, the cardinal passed over another aerial. "That one was taken at two hundred and fifty meters."

Reissen stared at the image with a confused look on his face. "So this barren spot is located in the middle of what looks like a lush forest."

"Precisely. This is why I would like you to go there and investigate it. We need to know why this is so. A simple quick in and out. Take some measurements, some pictures, whatever you think is necessary. Above all, I need your on-site psychic assessment. And, of course, whether it would be worth excavating."

"A solo investigation?"

A single head nod.

"But …"

"Dr. Reissen, dirt is, after all, dirt. What I want on my desk by week's end is your expert read and impressions on this site. It is hazardous? Does it need to be excavated? In short, should the Vatican step in? That sort of thing. I want you there tomorrow. See Father Joseph outside about your travel arrangements. He is quite good about organizing such things."

"Where is it located in Albania?"

"Just east of Tirana."

"Well, at least that's convenient."

"I thought that you would say that Dr. Reissen. *Gute Reise!*" the cardinal said as he stood up, signaling the meeting's conclusion.

Stunned and shell-shocked, Reissen quietly closed the cardinal's office door behind him only to find Father Joseph waiting for him. In his hand were several documents.

"*Professore* Reissen, here is your boarding pass and car reservation. Good hunting!"

Yes, he's new, but he's efficient.

*   *   *

Reissen's Alitalia flight the next day was a brief hour and a half. At the car rental kiosk, the Austrian selected something economical and four-wheel drive, because you just never knew. From the Tirana International Airport the drive to near the target site took about fifty minutes. Even with his GPS as a guide, he made several wrong turns. As it was, Reissen parked the rental on the side of a heavily forested road, and hiked into the woods, again using his handheld device.

The dense vegetation required an acrobat's agility to make way through the tangle of thorny bushes and tree roots. The archaeologist was glad he had chosen heavy clothing to wear. Still, he found himself picking off dozens of burrs. After several minutes, Reissen fell upon an overgrown path. A few quick brushes with his leather gloved hand revealed what it truly was—a stone pavement nearly three meters wide.

"Interesting," he murmured, "I wonder who built you and when?" As he studied his handheld, the Austrian decided to follow the road to his left, only occasionally stepping over invasive weeds and avoiding overhead brambles.

Following the old Roman road brought Reissen's heightened senses to life. His imagination freely played with how many it took to build it, how long, and above all, why here. Then, a curiosity appeared alongside the road, a rounded stone post, set upon a plinth, that together stood almost a meter and a half tall.

"What do we have here?"

After clearing away a thick and prickly vine covered with fragrant purple flowers, the archaeologist in Reissen smiled broadly. "A Roman milestone! By God I have found a Roman milestone!"

Rubbing his hand across its mossy surface, the Austrian could make out its Latin inscription:

GN. EGNATIUS
PRO COS VI
X
FECIT

which was repeated in Greek below. Translated, it said:

Gnaeus Egnatius
Governor for the sixth time
Mile Ten
Made This.

He took several pictures of the bilingual monument and its relationship to the paved road, then pulled out his notebook and recorded as best as he could both versions of the inscription. Reissen grinned ear-to-ear as he stuffed the notebook back into the zipper breast pocket of his jacket. Much like a little kid, he had stumbled upon an unexpected treasure.

Now with a decided jump in his step, and with his head on a swivel for other antiquities, Reissen continued on. After some one hundred meters, it was as if a curtain had been parted. The forest's thick vegetation gave way to a spectacularly desolate clearing dominated by a low mound in its center.

Witnessing this dramatic ecological change was one thing, experiencing the raw psychic energy bubble of the clearing was quite another, as it nearly brought the highly-sensitive archaeologist to his knees. A broad gamut of intense emotions pummeled Reissen. Pain, agony, utter hopelessness, coupled with a blinding rage, threatened to engulf him like a smothering wave.

Deeply shaken, Reissen slowed his progress along the ancient pavement to a crawl, as if walking in sticky honey. He trudged on, nonetheless, forcing himself ever deeper into the glen, inching his way closer to the mound.

The rocky and eroded hillock and its immediate environs were utterly devoid of life, something that in Reissen's experience, even the harsh Egyptian desert could not claim. A glance around provided a lush and forested green framework of dense beech and pine trees. This extreme dichotomy between death and life further disoriented the Austrian, to the point that when he had finally reached the eastern side of the mound, where the road approached at its nearest, he received a vision that dropped him to his knees. Its brutal impact caused tears to flow unbidden.

Directly in front of Reissen, the vision depicted the eastern portion of the mound stripped of its soil, exposing an entranceway. Men in ancient garb milled around as another, clad in priestly robes wearing Egyptian insignia and eye paint, placed the last stone, sealing the portal. Yet, an awful psychic resonance of sheer terror and desperate hopelessness emanated from the mound, which slammed into Reissen like a boxer's blow. The source was clear—someone had been left alive in the mound. At the priest's direction, a group of men quickly covered over the entrance with the surrounding piles of soil. That task completed, the priest then vigorously cursed the mound, spitting out his words with such a vengeance that spittle flew. The priest then tore apart a common snake, and anointed the freshly placed dirt with its blood.

When the vision cleared, the archaeologist's knees ached. Glancing down at his wristwatch, he saw why. He had been kneeling for more than twenty minutes. Emotionally spent from the vision, with dried salty trails of tears on his face, Reissen levered himself up, and briefly staggered. He took several photographs, turned around, and made his way back to the rental car.

"So the good cardinal sent me here to provide a psychic assessment." Reissen raggedly said once again among the trees. "Well damnit, I will sure give him one."

*   *   *

That week in his written report, the archaeologist stated, "It is as if someone treated the mound and its surroundings with a bleach or some other intensely caustic chemical."

His conclusion contained the following. "Without question, the central feature appears to be a tumulus, or burial site, which I am told are common throughout the region. As to why this site is so psychically-charged, only an excavation of the mound could answer. But before that can happen, we need to find someone who can remove an extremely powerful damnation spell. I strongly recommend that the site is investigated."

Reissen chose not to share his vision with the cardinal or in his report.

CHAPTER 3

Reissen's brief visit within the Albanian archaeological preserve occurred without anyone's notice. As ordered, the Austrian just slipped in, took some pictures, made some notes, and slipped out. Cardinal Alberti thought that such an approach, at least initially, was best. But now with the weight of the Reissen's written assessment in hand, the Vatican had to make their intentions known.

"*Përshëndetje*, this is Galaty," the professor answered in his native tongue.

"Professor Galaty, my name is Cardinal Alberti of the Vatican in Rome. How are you today, sir?"

The call frankly surprised Galaty. He had never before spoken with a Roman cardinal. But what really impressed the Albanian was the man was speaking French, Galaty's second language that went back to his graduate school days at the Sorbonne.

"Quite well," Galaty said easily shifting into a Parisian accent. "Why do I deserve this honor?"

"Professor Galaty, I have been asked by my superiors to initiate a cultural exchange program between your archaeological department and the Vatican's Gregorian Museum. Would your department welcome the overture of such an exchange?"

Mouth agape, Galaty did not know what to say at first, but based on his last departmental financial review with the university's administration, his interest became quite real. He had been faced with either halting the restoration of the late Roman mountain fortifications, or the loss of funding for four graduate student assistantships. The former represented the cessation of three years of work; the latter openly threatened the future of his department's graduate student program. The loss of either would hurt the department's reputation, but he had chosen to shut down the restoration effort at the close of this season in order to preserve the department's future—a truly draconian choice. Consequently, any outside source of funding for his department and its research efforts independent of the greedy hands of the university administration, Galaty would enthusiastically embrace.

"Cardinal Alberti, my department would indeed 'welcome such an overture.' How do you suggest we proceed?"

"Perhaps I send to you one of our representatives, an archaeologist perhaps? Then, the two of you can discuss all the options."

"That would be acceptable," Galaty choked out,

not wishing to appear too eager.

"Marvelous. The archaeologist I wish to send is Professor Dr. Erik Gerhard Reissen. He is an Egyptologist and formerly of the University of Vienna. Would that be acceptable?"

"We would be honored to have him as our guest."

"Wonderful. I suspect that the two of you will have much to discuss. May I send Dr. Reissen to you next week?"

Galaty glanced about frantically searching for his day planner, found it, and saw that week was open. "Absolutely, Cardinal Alberti. Just kindly send me the man's itinerary and we will take care of the rest. Here is my email address."

After recording the departmental chairman's information, Alberti concluded. "Splendid. Good day, Dr. Galaty."

Quite frankly, Galaty, a devote Muslim, could only conclude by the end of the Vatican's phone call that the goddess Fortuna, in its true pagan sense, had just made a visitation. And this Dr. Reissen he knew well by his reputation alone, as an experienced archaeologist. A quick glance to his office's bookshelf was proof enough. For two of the man's books were there, not to mention his recent television appearance.

*   *   *

Cardinal Alberti smiled at the seated Austrian opposite him as he hung up the phone. "Dr. Reissen, I expect you to broker this cultural exchange in a fair and reasonable manner."

"Understood, Cardinal Alberti. What's my budget?"

The question caused the cleric to pause, again noting the man's penchant for directness.

"Your past experience of directing several Egyptian archaeological efforts should provide you with a 'fair and reasonable' sense of what is required. Just do not pawn off St. Peter," Alberti ended with a sly smile.

*   *   *

Reissen expected to receive several things from his visit—institutional cordiality, collegial warmth, and the pushback of an immensely proud Islamic university culture. Here, as a Vatican representative, he was the Great Satan. That meant he had to tread on eggshells. As a consequence, the Austrian expected that his initial offer would be welcomed, discussed, but ultimately rejected. Reissen knew it would take all his experience in his dealings with the politics and hidden landmines of the Egyptian Supreme Council of Antiquities. He did, however, have an ace up his sleeve. Cardinal Alberti managed to ferret out the state of Galaty's departmental finances. When Reissen asked how he had come across such information, the cardinal smiled and said, "There is little that the Holy See does not know."

* * *

After he had scanned the barcode on Reissen's passport, the customs agent wanted to know why he had returned to Tirana so soon. The Austrian just shrugged and said, "I like your city and its university. In fact, just outside someone from the university should be there to pick me up."

That answer seemed to do as the entry stamp was applied to his passport with a thump. The agent grunted, returned it, and waved him through as he was already visually assessing the next person in line.

* * *

When Galaty met Reissen at the airport, he had little trouble recognizing him as he emerged through the sliding doors of the customs area. He had the look— worn work boots, care-worn tan pants, open-collared shirt, and sweat-stained bush hat. Over one shoulder hung a similarly distressed backpack. The man came light. But it was Reissen's stature, fitness, tanned skin, and energetic step that screamed "dirt archaeologist" to the departmental chair. The fact that Galaty recognized his face from the television documentaries was purely secondary.

Galaty stood stock still in the greeting crowd as he unnecessarily held a white placard before him that said "DR. REISSEN." Perhaps it was whimsy, but Galaty wanted to be as hospitable as possible, while hiding his obvious awareness of just who Reissen was and what he might represent to his department's future.

*   *   *

Once beyond the customs area, Reissen slowed to see if anyone looked like a Professor Galaty, department chairman of archaeology and history. And there he was, off to one side, a short and fit man wearing an open tweed sports jacket, tan slacks, and a magnificent salt and pepper moustache that matched his thick head of unruly hair. It helped that he held a placard with his name emblazoned across it.

"Hello, Professor Dr. Galaty. I am Reissen," the Austrian declared in flawless French, as he bowed slightly and extended his hand. A firm and warm one greeted it, full of calluses, full of hope.

"Welcome to my country, Professor Dr. Reissen. It is indeed a pleasure. Please follow me to my car."

En route to the man's parked vehicle, Galaty casually asked, "Where do you wish to begin, Professor Dr. Reissen? To meet the departmental staff or tour our recent archaeological restoration project?"

"The restoration project, Professor Dr. Galaty. I am not a bureaucrat, but an archaeologist. And, by the way, my first name is Erik. Please use it."

Opening the passenger side door, Galaty smiled, "Alright … Erik … the restoration project it is."

As Galaty weaved his way through the airport's traffic, he delivered a brief travelogue of this and that as Reissen rested his arm on the open door sill in the warm sunshine.

Waiting for an opening in this nervously delivered listing of facts and figures, the Austrian asked, "Tell me about this archaeological restoration project of yours professor."

Now breaking away from the congested traffic, Galaty did so, now with much more enthusiasm, telling his tale of impassioned discovery, survey, and progress.

"Just imagine, Erik, uncovering literally hundreds

of meters of crenellated curtain wall! It was all there waiting to be found, buried under a thick layer of overgrown holly oak bushes."

"How tall are these walls?"

A shrug, then, "Anywhere between five to eight meters depending upon the topography."

"Did you find any gates?"

"Oh, my yes! And sally ports too! No intact gates or doorways mind you, but their archways are there for all to see."

"Are these casemate walls, professor?"

"Yes, and no. Not casemate construction as one might find in the ancient Near East, rather, late Roman casemate construction with a poured slurry of cement in its core that binds together a rubble fill. Very durable."

So the conversation continued, with an Egyptologist trying to better understand a Late Roman restoration project, while getting a read on its passionate investigator. But when Reissen ran out of questions to ask, he said, "So, professor, when will this project come to completion? Surely it will make a fine tourist attraction, much like the Great Wall of China."

With that question, the effervescent chairman stopped dead and pursed his lips. "Sadly no Erik. My funding has been cut off by my university."

"*What?* Are they insane?"

"Of that, I have often wondered. But the administration *did* give me a choice. Either fund the restoration project or fund four graduate students. I chose the students."

Reissen was surprised at the chairman's candor, which matched what Cardinal Alberti had told him precisely. The Austrian's conclusion: *Galaty was a straight shooter.* So Reissen changed the subject.

"Are there any other archaeological sites in the area worthy of investigation?"

Now Reissen noticed that the chairman gripped the steering wheel of his old Mercedes very tightly. "Yes … there is one that I have most recently taken a look at. It may be an Illyrian mound burial. But I am not sure." Then with an apologetic smile and a cock of his head, "Perhaps someday."

"You never know, Professor Galaty, that 'someday' may be tomorrow," Reissen said casually as he looked out the window.

At that, the Albanian pulled his car over to the side of the road. He stared at the Austrian. "What precisely do you mean?"

"Well, for starters, a portion of your graduate school budget could be transferred to the Gregorian

Museum, where your students would receive an enriching research experience. That should take some of the strain off of your departmental finances. Secondly, depending upon what I see of your restoration effort, further cultural funding may be available. What's your best estimate on the restoration's completion?"

"Two years."

"At what cost?"

"About forty thousand *leks*."

Reissen pulled out his smart device and began typing, "In other words, about three hundred and ten to three hundred and forty Euros per season."

"In round figures."

"Professor, I cannot imagine how insulting it was for you to be forced to decide between the continuation of an ongoing project—nearing completion, and the future of your graduate program."

The two men locked eyes. Much was exchanged.

"Professor, I think you should show me those fortifications that you love so much."

*   *   *

The Albanian archaeological camp consisted of used military wall tents with wooden floors. Six tents were devoted to artifact restoration and storage, the main tent comprised of mostly pottery fragments, along with some bits of paraphernalia—spear points, arrow heads, nails, and the occasional coin. Three joined tents made up the kitchen and "cafeteria" for the locally sourced laborers and university staff. There were no on-site overnight accommodations. Four military surplus diesel generators provided power. Everywhere Reissen looked there was no wastage that he could detect. If anything, Galaty's entire glorious restoration project was taking place on a shoestring and was proceeding successfully.

Now sitting in the cafeteria for lunch after a grand tour of the walls, gates, and the centralized ruins of a Roman military camp, Reissen commented on how good the food was.

"Thank you, Erik. Would you like to meet our cook?"

Surprised, but at the same time delighted, the Austrian said he would. So Galaty got up and disappeared into the kitchen area, only to reemerge with a short stocky woman with her graying hair gathered under a head cloth.

In Reissen's eyes, this charming woman glowed with energy and her radiant smile seemed to light up the mess area. The Austrian stood to greet the two.

With great formality Galaty made his introduction in his native tongue. "*Gjyshe* Ajola, this is Professor Dr. Erik Reissen from the Vatican. He told me that he wanted to meet the cook, because he was so impressed with our lunch."

It was an awkward moment. *Gjyshe* Ajola wrung her hands, while Reissen gave her a short bow. But all of that went away when the Austrian reached out and grasped her hands and their eyes met. Both were surprised by the power of the warm psychic connection.

Reissen just broadly smiled, as did she, while the pair communicated at a furious rate during the time it took to blink an eye. The Austrian broke the bond, thanking the woman in French, which Galaty—completely oblivious of the bonding—unnecessarily translated for the cook.

As the cook made her way back to the kitchen, she turned, smiled warmly and waved back. Reissen just stood there, acknowledged the wave, returned it, and reseated himself.

"She is quite a cook," Reissen finally managed.

"Indeed, she is. She keeps this project together with her delicious food." Galaty proudly added, "Our morale is quite high because of it."

Reissen then asked, "So, what's your budget for

publishing this fine project of yours?"

"As of the recent financial review, none," Galaty stated gloomily.

The Austrian just shook his head in total disbelief.

"What about its annual maintenance once the project is completed?"

Another head shake.

"So, Lorenc, when are you going to show me this Illyrian mound you mentioned?"

*   *   *

"Erik, please notice that the Roman road we are standing on curves around the mound in the center of this forest glen," Lorenc pointed out. "If that mound is artificial, as I firmly believe it is, then that alone dates the mound to the Iron Age."

"Why do you say that?"

"Because this road was built during the second century BC by the Roman governor of the region—a man named Gnaeus Egnatius. Since its course rounds the mound, it must therefore be pre-second century BC in date."

"Interesting," Reissen murmured while trying to conceal his absolute psychic aversion to the place.

"How long have you known about this site?"

"Only about a month. Our cook was the one who found it."

"That cheerful grandmother?"

"Yes, indeed.

"Lorenc, can I assume that the cost of this mound's investigation is not in your budget either?"

"You are correct."

"What would you say if the Gregorian Museum was willing to do a package deal?"

"'Package deal?' Whatever do you mean Erik?"

"Let us imagine the following. The institution of a graduate student exchange for two students per year to the Gregorian Museum, where they would undertake their research within the museum, and have their food and board paid for."

"That would be wonderful, Erik!"

"I am not finished," the Austrian indicated with an upraised finger. "Secondly, let us imagine that the Gregorian Museum will fully fund the final two years of the late Roman wall system's restoration, plus two years of maintenance thereafter, plus sufficient funding for its publication."

Lorenc just stood there mouth agape.

"Now for the good part," Reissen said while pointing at the mound opposite, "that needs immediate attention and that too the Gregorian Museum is willing to fully fund."

"Why immediately, Erik?"

"Because my friend, that is a cultural liability just waiting to be robbed. I have seen this situation play out countless times in Egypt. Just imagine what it might contain."

Now wide-eyed, "Potentially, an Illyrian noble burial," Galaty gushed.

"Precisely. Now, Lorenc, can your department undertake such an investigation alone? Do you have the manpower?"

"No. We are stretched thin as it is with the restoration project. What do you propose?"

"A cooperative alliance. I am very concerned about the security of that mound and the Gregorian Museum has resources. But just for a moment imagine, Lorenc, if that burial is intact. Do you have the personnel to clear it?"

This time a sad shake of the head.

"What about enlisting the help of your university's fine arts department? Surely they would love to restore and care for the glittering bronze burial equipment of an Illyrian noble."

"I am not so sure, Erik. Departmental politics at the

university can be quite heated."

"It is all about finances, is it not?"

"Sadly, yes. We all compete for a small portion of the annual budget."

"But if the finances are supplied by an external source, then what is stopping your two departments from working together?"

Now nodding, "Good point, and Professor Grillo is a fine colleague," the Albanian said with a nod.

"One last thing," the Austrian said.

"What is that?"

"What if that the Illyrian burial has been disturbed? It is just a suspicion, of course, a situation that happens all too often in Egypt. But when that mound burial is opened, I want to be here to see it. For if my suspicions are indeed correct, there might be an intrusive burial within it that you and your department will not want to deal with."

Frowning, "Erik, you are beginning to sound like our superstitious cook, *Gjyshe* Ajola."

"Perhaps I am, Lorenc. Perhaps I am. So Lorenc, do we have an agreement?"

His answer was two hands heartily shaking as one.

* * *

As with so many things, the devil is always in the details, even on goodwill, handshake agreements. As expected, the university administration guardedly welcomed the financial infusion from the Vatican, but demanded total control of the funds' disbursement. This the Vatican firmly, but diplomatically, refused. Meanwhile, within the Albanian university community, raging storms blew over the overreaching administration, academic freedom, and the blocking of inter-departmental cooperative efforts. In the end, it came down to the greasing of several university administrators' palms before the exchange and multiple funding agreements were formalized. Further, during the convoluted negotiations, the name of the exchange program and its funding was changed to bolster several egos. It became known as The Albanian-Vatican Cultural Assistance Program. Additionally, the exchange itself was expanded to four graduate students *per annum*.

CHAPTER 4

Fourth months later, with the cultural exchange program established and in motion, Reissen returned to Albania now as a *bona fide* Vatican representative. Several colleagues also arrived with the Austrian. Sister Mary Gabriella—a member of the Pro Deo paranormal faculty, and two graduate students in archaeology.

Sophia Lorenzo was a Late Roman ceramics expert, who was immediately welcomed by the overworked restoration staff and put to work. Lorenzo, a powerful empath, fit in like an old shoe among the piles of shattered shards.

Geoffrey Smith, an experienced field photographer, accompanied the Reissen-led tour of the mound, which provided orientation, but mostly allowed Sister Gabriella—all four foot eleven of her, an opportunity to experience its oppressive psychic bubble.

"Saints preserve us all!" the psychic nun exclaimed upon entering the meadow. "You were not kidding one bit Erik. This is indeed dangerous, dark magic." Upon reaching the mound itself, the one-eyed nun commented as she walked around its perimeter. "I sense a curse, an old one, very powerful. What I do not understand is its source of animation. I will have to check the regional ley lines. Perhaps the conjurer tapped into one."

Hearing this, Smith started snapping images of the mound. His Canon digital SLR gave off simulated shutter sounds.

"Do you think the curse can be lifted, sister?" Reissen asked.

"Theoretically, all spells can be nullified. About this one, I am not sure. Can you remember any outstanding details about what you saw in that vision of yours?"

Reissen rubbed his forehead, "The Egyptian priest was very agitated as he recited the spell, which I thought was in a Latin dialect. But when the priest finished, he tore a snake in half and sprinkled the mound's entrance with its blood, just like a Roman Catholic priest would use an incense burner or *aspergillum*—a holy water sprinkler."

As Sister Gabriella listened, she frowned deeply. "Erik, I will have to return to Rome immediately. I recall a manuscript that mentions the use of snake blood in such a manner.

More shutter sounds echoed from Smith's camera, while he listened in on the conversation.

"Now Erik, you said that the Egyptian priest was agitated. What precisely do you mean by that?"

"His body shook with hate as he literally spat out the words of the spell."

"Hmm. Was he barefoot?"

"Yes."

"That was how he jump-started this spell! He expended his own personal reserve, while simultaneously linked directly to the ground. That priest tapped a ley line to power this spell. Of that, I am now quite certain."

Reissen nodded in understanding at the sister's conclusion.

"Erik, I will return to Rome on this evening's flight. What I have seen is sufficient. I will keep in touch with you about any developments. By the way Erik, your knowledge of liturgical objects is quite impressive. Are you perhaps considering joining the clergy?"

"That is very doubtful sister."

"Pity. You would make such a fine one."

"Thank you, sister," Reissen said, getting the conversation back on track. "Anything you can do to lift this god-awful oppression would be much appreciated."

Sister Gabriella patted the Austrian's arm, "Erik, be assured, I will do my very best."

During this entire conversation, Smith listened intently. Finally he mustered the courage to ask, "Dr. Reissen, just what was your vision about?"

Reissen looked at him and said stonily, "The burial of a man, who was still alive."

"Good *God!*" Smith breathed.

"Indeed. Now let us get back to the archaeological base camp. And by the way, none of this is to be shared with any of our Albanian colleagues. Am I clear?"

Two emphatic nods.

*   *   *

Reissen waited two full days before beginning the investigation of the mound, while hoping for Sister Gabriella to come up with a solution to lift its curse. So far, nothing but silence from the Vatican, and in the Austrian's mind, that was not encouraging.

But first things first, Reissen and Smith, with Galaty and several newly hired laborers in tow, returned to the clearing to create an official photographic record and take its measurements before any spade broke soil.

The Austrian had to contain his surprise when Galaty performed his survey using only knotted cords and wooden stakes. While the methodology was sound, he also realized just how spoiled he had become with modern laser-based equipment. So ended day one, with a rough survey map completed and many photos taken.

On the hike back to the base camp, Reissen asked Smith, "Did you notice anything out of the ordinary today?"

"Other than their absolutely ancient survey technique?"

"Yes, other than that."

"My digital imagery lacks focus. Try as I might, there is always a blurry quality to my mound shots—especially along its eastern side. The western side shots are, well, adequate, but the eastern side is trash."

"That's very interesting Geoffrey. Why do you suppose that is?"

"Well, Erik, most likely the source of that curse Sister Gabriella is working on."

"And why do you say that?"

"Several of our colleagues back home are working on measuring the physical effects of electromagnetism on digital imagery."

"Really?"

"Yeah. Apparently strong fields can distort a digital image. The question is—what is doing all the distortion? Is it occurring within the digital hardware, in essence, the chips, or with the object itself?"

"Are you saying that magic is nothing more than a strong magnetic field?"

A shrug, then, "Sort of. Think of it this way. To exist magnetic fields need a source of power—some sort of energy. Gifted psychics can support that power short-term, while ley lines have sufficient energy for the long-term. The breaking or lifting of spells then, in essence, is a grounding or diversion of a power source."

"Huh."

"But to get to the real nitty-gritty, is to examine the phenomenon at the quantum level. That's where a lot of stuff is going on—stuff that we have yet to figure out."

"So, to summarize, the chips in your camera are being messed with at the quantum level."

"Yes, that is it precisely—the stronger the spell, the greater the optical distortion."

*   *   *

That evening Reissen finally received word from Sister Gabriella.

"Okay Erik, here is what we are up against. That Egyptian priest invoked a personalized execration spell or curse that damned the inhabitant of the mound and immediate surroundings. Sound familiar?"

"All too much. The Egyptian magician Djedi's tomb was full of such curses."

"But what is intriguing here Erik, is that the priest did not break an inscribed inanimate object like a bowl or jar to execute the spell. Instead, he ritualistically tore apart a living snake. Erik, did that snake have any writing or symbols painted on it?"

"I do not recall, just that it looked like a common spotted snake."

"Well, my guess is that some of those spots were hieroglyphs. And if so, then to sacrifice something living, to initiate a spell, only focuses and magnifies its outcome."

"*Mein Gott!*"

"Indeed. Unfortunately, the reversal of such a spell will require the generation of substantial energy to cancel it out, and, a commensurate amount of life."

The phone line went silent on Reissen's end.

"Are you still there, Erik?"

"Yes I am, sister. How much is 'commensurate'?"

"The use of another snake. I would assume at least a meter long will do, decorated with the appropriate symbols."

"Oh. Can I help out in any way?"

"No, Erik, that will not be necessary. I have

already sourced the reptile and will paint the creation text on it myself."

"What will be the medium?"

"A sample of the snake's own blood, ground ash, and olive oil, of course."

"When should we expect your return?"

"Tomorrow morning. Will you pick me up?"

"Gladly. When do you arrive?"

"On the 9:35 am Alitalia flight."

*　　*　　*

Reissen told Galaty that the photographer needed more time at the site, explaining the man had experienced a technical issue, which required new parts shipped in from Rome. This delayed the start of the mound's excavation by two days, thereby creating a window when Sister Gabriella could perform her magic.

At high noon the next day, the diminutive nun, dressed in stark white vestments with a garland of fragrant flowers around her neck and head, invoked the counter spell. Barefoot, she wriggled her toes deep into the sterile soil nearest the still hidden eastern entranceway. Holding a large snake before her, Sister Gabriella sang a melodious Latin verse while gently swaying to its rhythm.

Life, life, life is to be again granted to this place.
For too long it has been denied its place.
Hathor breathe life back into that, which has been
denied your sweetness.

This chant the nun sang three times, after which she bent down and released the serpent. As it crawled away across the parched and desolate landscape, all that it touched turned green and began blooming in profusion. Much like the seepage of water, the snake's path widened and grew outward, creating a lush ground cover of grasses and flowers long held so unjustly dormant. As this inundating flood of life approached the mound, it began spreading along its base and once surrounded, began its slow ascent. During this rebirth of life, the heavy psychic bubble of gloom retreated with every green blade of grass until it was gone.

When Reissen came to the nun's side, he found her panting from exertion, her chest heaving. Streams of sweat poured down her face.

"Help me, Erik. I am exhausted."

From deep within the dark recesses of the mound a rustling occurred.

* * *

The following morning Reissen took a greatly refreshed Sister Gabriella to the airport.

"Thank you yet again sister. You have really made my job more tolerable."

"Nonsense, Erik. I was just doing *my* job. Now," the nun said while patting the Austrian's hand, "go do *yours*."

The next day the mound's excavation began in earnest. During the past eighteen, however, the forest clearing and its mound had been transformed into a breathtakingly verdant and colorful lawn. Bees buzzed between the many wild flowers. Crickets jumped. Deer casually grazed along one edge on the sweet grass.

"What has happened here?" Galaty wanted to know.

"Do you believe in miracles, Lorenc?"

The short and proud man stood there looking around with his hands on hips, his head shaking in disbelief. "I do not know," his eyes full of wonder.

"Is not the Vatican's financial assistance a miracle of sorts?"

"Why yes, of course it is. But, Erik, this is simply astounding."

"Yes, indeed it is. It is a reminder to us all that we have much to be thankful for."

"Which God are you thanking?" the Moslem pointedly asked.

"Does it really matter?" Reissen smiled.

"No, I suppose it does not."

"So, my friend, shall we begin?"

"I must admit that I feel sad about digging into this glorious groundcover," Galaty said, spreading his arms wide.

"And that is why I never learned to play golf," the Austrian said with a chuckle.

The two archaeologists laid out a long and narrow partition of stakes and twine that equally divided the mound in two. The two reasoned this elongated trench would reveal the tiny hill's stratigraphy from the top to its bottom. That was the plan.

Four laborers began by scraping away three to four centimeters of earth with their flat-bladed trenching tools. This spoil was then screened in a wooden a-frame contraption, as one of Galaty's graduate students looked for any cultural artifacts or faunal remains.

Before the workmen encountered the fitted stone blocks of the tumulus' dome, they found not one, but two shallow graves. The stone cists, rectangular boxes constructed of thin stone slabs, contained the skeletons of two individuals. The interments Galaty quickly dated to the early Byzantine period, specifically to the reign of the Emperor Tiberius II, based upon the silver coins found wedged into their eye sockets. Around each skull, a leather, belt-like strap had once covered over the eyes.

Then Reissen shooed the laborers away, before the digging went any further, as he and Galaty squatted over the remains.

"Lorenc, I am going to request a forensic expert from the Vatican."

"Why, Erik?"

"Look beyond your precious silver coins, my friend," as the Austrian brushed away some loose soil from before the skull. "Look at the upper and lower canine teeth of this individual."

The Albanian covered his mouth in shock.

"As if that is not sufficient, carefully examine the stone slabs that covered these graves. Note the extensive grooving on their interior surfaces. Now look at the heavy wear on the bones of their fingertips. These individuals were buried alive."

Galaty just looked in disbelief from the scratched slabs and back to the skeletons. His eyes went wide with incredulity. His face turned white. "That explains the odd leather head strap on each …"

"Lorenc, with your permission, I am going to clear these remains myself, and bag and tag them for further study at the Vatican. Do you agree?"

A vigorous nod.

The next day the team returned and Galaty seemed gloomy.

"What's the matter, Lorenc?"

"Those two bodies. They trouble me."

"They trouble me as well."

"Erik."

"Yes."

"Thank you for your quick thinking regarding the laborers. We do not need unnecessary panic or publicity. I thank you again for suggesting their removal."

So the archaeologists continued and soon reached the carefully cut and placed blocks of the mound's dome.

"Lorenc, we now have our proof. This hillock is indeed artificial."

"What now, Erik?"

"Its entrance, which side should we begin with? I personally favor the eastern side."

"Why not? It makes sense. It faces the rising sun." the Albanian agreed.

Staking out a generous three square meters with the knotted twine on a side, the pair began again.

Choosing to communicate with the laborers

through his colleague Galaty, Reissen once again instructed them to scrap away the topsoil in three centimeter passes with their flat-bladed trenching tools. Once again they collected the spoil and one of Galaty's students screened it in the wooden a-frame contraption. Other than dirt, little of cultural value was identified. But as they dug deeper and deeper, the outline of an arched entrance appeared. Digging further, a large shattered ceramic container was found.

"Why do you think this amphora is here?" Galaty wanted to know.

"Part of the burial ceremony?" Reissen guessed. "The spilling of an entire wine amphora to please the gods of the Underworld? Who knows?"

Calling a halt to the progress, Reissen beckoned to Smith to officially record their find with meter sticks for scale. Just as the amphora's upper body fragments were removed, a small skeleton was discovered nestled within the crushed remains of the massive storage container.

"Smith, record this with scale," Reissen beckoned.

"Gladly. What do you think it is?"

"Looks like a small rodent," he said, and carefully removed the delicate remains and placed them within a numbered plastic Ziploc bag. "We will only know for sure, once a forensic expert joins us."

With the amphora cleared, and in a moment of prescient diplomacy, the Austrian had Galaty and his laborers gather in front of the mound. Toothy and toothless, they unashamedly grinned back into Smith's camera lens to be preserved for posterity.

"How is the focus now?" the archaeologist asked his photographer under his breath.

"Outstanding professor."

"Glad to hear it."

*　　*　　*

By mid-afternoon, the archaeological team had fully-exposed the mound's arched entranceway. Pleased as punch over their efforts, Galaty asked Reissen, "How did you know that the entranceway was on the eastern side?"

"Just a guess. But your argument for it facing the east convinced me," the Austrian said as he offered his hand, which Galaty gladly took.

"I look forward to tomorrow's break in."

"Careful Lorenc. Tomorrow may hold more than what you wish for."

CHAPTER 5

That same afternoon Reissen called his superior, Cardinal Alberti, in Rome.

"*Ciao*, Dr. Reissen. How goes your investigations?"

"Very well, Your Eminence. Tomorrow we will break into the mound. But before we do, I anticipate the immediate need for a forensics expert."

"How immediate?"

"On tomorrow's early flight to Tirana."

"Understood. I will see what I can do. You can expect my email with his itinerary within the hour."

"Thank you, Your Eminence."

*   *   *

Dr. Giuseppe Largo was on the next morning's flight. A youthful bundle of energy with a runner's lean and tallish build, the forensic scientist was on loan to the Vatican from the University of Rome. Regardless, Reissen shook his head in amazement once again at the long reach of that Christian institution.

"Is this your first archaeological assignment, Dr. Largo?" the Austrian asked as a pang of jealousy squeezed at the Austrian's heart, as he drove the fit young man in gold wire-rimmed glasses and a dark curly mop of hair from the airport to the mound's dig site.

"Yes, Dr. Reissen, this is indeed my first, and I am quite excited about participating in it." Largo enthused, the knees of his long legs resting against the car's dashboard.

"Well, I am pleased to hear that, but one word of warning my young colleague, archaeology can be quite grisly."

"What do you mean?"

"Already we have recovered two anomalous individuals. Today, we are about to open a sealed tomb. But we might encounter multiple burials, perhaps even intrusive ones. We need you to make that determination and to sort out any intrusionary deposits from the tomb's original remains."

"What do you anticipate will be the state of the remains?"

"Unknown, but expect anything from pure skeletal all the way to fully-mummified."

The young scientist's eyebrows rose as he paused to absorb the ramifications of Reissen's statement.

"How are you with non-human skeletal remains?"

"Reasonably good."

A positive grunt.

"Another item, Dr. Largo. Whatever we find is confidential. Are you aware of that?"

"Yes. I have already signed all the legal paperwork with the Vatican," he answered with a serious tone.

"Good. One final thing, you might be asked to personally deliver some remains to the Vatican."

"I have been informed about that as well. Cardinal Alberti told me the archaeological laboratory at the Gregorian Museum will take whatever I bring back."

*   *   *

Galaty, ever the gentleman, had nonetheless waited impatiently with his men for Reissen and the Vatican forensics expert to arrive at the mound. Even though they appeared several minutes before ten in the morning, Galaty remained hopping around from one foot to another like a kid before a Christmas tree loaded with presents.

"Erik, how should we begin?" the Albanian eagerly asked, crowbar in hand, ready and raring to go.

"Easily enough Lorenc, with the upper blocks of the entranceway. By the way, may I introduce Dr. Giuseppe Largo, a forensic expert on loan to us from the University of Rome."

After several nods and handshakes, Largo stepped back and took his place to one side, while Reissen and Galaty approached the entranceway, each armed with crowbars, with pure chaos and mayhem in mind.

The Austrian pointed, "That one looks promising." The work began in earnest, but the blocks proved to be stubborn, but after much grunting, prying, and several colorful curses, the first loosened, and fell to the ground with a heavy thud.

The removed block, a stone about fifteen inches square, left a dark shadow in the entranceway's wall. Galaty peaked in the gap and immediately started gagging. Staggering away and covering his mouth, the archaeological director just barely made it to one side before he threw up.

"Post-mortem gas," Largo said to Reissen with absolute certainty. "Allow the chamber to vent. Perhaps remove several more blocks to speed the process."

No one touched anything for the next three hours. When they resumed, Reissen took the lead this time and dismantled the entire upper section of the entranceway before Galaty took over again to complete the job.

Once again however, the unlucky archaeological director discovered something unexpected. At the base of the entranceway's interior, Galaty found the remains of an adult in a fetal position, partially skeleton, partially desiccated into a near-mummified condition.

"Smith, record this with scale."

While the photographer did his job, Reissen waved Largo over. "This is your third subject to take back to Rome. Like the others, I want a full forensic workup."

"Understood, Dr. Reissen."

Then the Austrian turned to Galaty. "This body is an intrusive burial, if not a sacrifice. This is precisely what I was worried about finding. Do I have your permission to remove it for study back at the Vatican?"

Visibly shaken, "Absolutely Erik. I had no idea."

Then Reissen had a thought. "How well do you know your cook?"

A shrug, "Not well."

"She found this mound, did she not?"

"Yes."

"Why?"

At first the archaeological director looked away while he gathered his thoughts.

"*Gjyshe* Ajola told me that the clearing, and the mound in particular, had troubled her greatly—even to the point of causing her sleepless nights and nightmares."

Reissen listened carefully to his colleague's

revelation and sensed the pain in his admission.

"I see, Lorenc. Thank you for telling me this. But beware, my dear colleague, this mound may contain more surprises."

"Like what?"

"The potential for more intrusive burials."

"How do you know this Erik?" Galaty asked with frustration and accusatory eyes.

"Because Lorenc, like your cook, I too felt the utter evil of this archaeological site. And the source of that 'wrongness' is not this poor wretch's body." Reissen pointed. "We will encounter more. Mark my words."

The Albanian listened, nodded, and asked. "Just how important is it Erik, that we excavate this mound?"

"To your department, the Illyrian remains will make your university famous and put your department on the map. To the Vatican, I suspect any other intrusive remains that we might find will be important, if not epoch-making."

"Really? How so?"

"Evidence, proof of the supernatural, of myth, of that which has always frightened men's souls. Lorenc, do you trust me?"

"I do not see any reason not to," the man said frankly.

"Before we continue clearing this tomb, I would strongly suggest that you dismiss your laborers again. What we may encounter might frighten them."

Casually glancing over in their direction, the archaeological director saw the four sitting on their excavation tools, chatting, and smoking cigarettes. "I agree Erik."

* * *

By mid-afternoon and with the four laborers retasked to the late Roman wall renovation, Largo had the fetal corpse collected, bagged, and recorded.

"Dr. Reissen, I have some preliminary observations that I think you should know about."

Reissen waved over Galaty and then said to the forensic expert, "Dr. Largo, tell us both about your 'preliminary observations'."

"First, that body was murdered, or sacrificed. He died of a slit throat."

Galaty's face turned a pasty white.

"And second, my preliminary finds indicate that the victim was partially eaten, especially the fingers, ears, face, and toes."

Galaty's eyes glazed over and Reissen reached out to steady the man.

"Gentlemen, the final word on this victim will have to wait until a full autopsy and laboratory workup are completed in Rome. Regardless, I will stand by my preliminary observations."

"Thank you Dr. Largo. I knew I could depend on you."

Reissen then escorted the two men over to the open entranceway, now cleared of its body. Flipping on his powerful LED flashlight, the three men peered deep into the mound's tomb. There, in its very center, surrounded by rodent bones, was a body grotesquely stretched out, held in place with ropes. The wrists and ankles shackled. The head held in some sort of an odd harness.

Galaty gagged at the sight. "*Gjyshe* Ajola was right!" he exclaimed. "Such a horrific scene. How could anyone commit such an inhuman act?"

Smith began the process and went to work recording several distinct items. The first task was to record the flooring of the circular tomb covered with small animal bones. One quite literally could not take a step without crushing them.

Next, Smith addressed the center of the tomb, which was dramatically taken up with a tall, outstretched partial skeleton shackled to the bedrock flooring. That grisly job done, Smith turned over the clearance of the central remains to Largo, who first collected the myriad of rodent remains, each in their own numbered bags.

"Do I have your permission to clear this poor wretch?" Reissen asked.

"By Allah's gray beard, yes!"

"That Dr. Largo," Reissen said with a deep sigh, "needs to be cleared today and taken to Rome." After Largo was finished, he approached the two head archaeologists shaking his head.

"Gentlemen, my preliminary analysis is that this last individual was horribly tortured and sacrificed *alive*—to be eaten by all of these rodents."

At the news, Galaty, deeply shaken, crossed his arms and demanded, "How do you know he was eaten alive?"

"By the nibble marks on the subject's long bones."

The Albanian just shook his head.

"Further," Largo continued, "this individual has huge upper canines. If I had to guess, gentlemen, I would identify this as the remains of a vampire."

Turning to the Albanian and pointing into the tomb, the Austrian said, "Lorenc, that is what so troubled your cook."

"Yes, yes, it now all makes sense," Galaty said while rubbing his forehead nervously.

Reissen then re-entered the tomb with Galaty.

Now panning the powerful beam along the rest of the tomb, the disturbed grave goods of an Illyrian nobleman's burial could be seen roughly pushed aside. Finely wrought bronze weaponry, pottery, jewelry, and the heady glint of gold could be seen everywhere.

"Lorenc, do you see all of that?"

"Indeed I do Erik."

"All of that, my friend, is yours to photograph, clear, preserve and restore, and publish."

"Erik, there is so much …"

"Yes, there is. It would be the prize of any museum. And now it is in your capable hands instead of appearing on the black market."

*   *   *

Two days later, one very shook up field photographer frantically called Reissen.

"I am very sorry, Professor Reissen, but all of the field imagery of the tall skeleton did not expose correctly," the Vatican photographer nervously tried to explain over the phone.

"And what of the site's other skeletons Geoffrey?

Are they all ruined as well?" the Austrian queried with a raised eyebrow.

"Oh, everything else exposed correctly, professor."

"I see. Can you send me these incorrectly exposed images?"

"Yes, professor. I will do so immediately."

Four minutes later, Reissen's laptop chimed. As the archaeologist scanned the twelve suspect images, he had to smile to himself. The photographer, a good one, had missed one crucial detail. The heavy ropes that had stretched the tall skeleton were captured in the imagery clear as day, but appeared to be suspended in the air, connected to nothing. This detail he decided not to point out to the distressed photographer, who had only fixated upon the missed skeletal material.

Indeed Reissen understood the reason for this all too well. Once before he had encountered such camera shy and non-photogenic remains at the Egyptian magician's Djedi tomb. Such missing images of human artifacts were a tell-tale of a lost soul, or perhaps better said, that total lack thereof. That this tall skeleton could not be photographed therefore, did not surprise him. If anything, it confirmed his darkest suspicions—it was indeed a vampire, an entity devoid of anything like a soul.

CHAPTER 6

As soon as Dr. Largo delivered the remains of the four bodies to the Gregorian Museum, a team of forensic specialists leapt into action. Unlike Dr. Largo, who typically dealt with more common mortal issues like murder, car accidents, disease, and the like, these "specialists" worked principally on the analysis of paranormal phenomena and cryptid entities. As a consequence, the analysis on three of the four bodies produced nothing short of jaw-dropping results. Even these relatively jaded specialists found themselves astonished and recognized they stood on the cusp of making paranormal forensic history.

Several days later the team's final report lay on Cardinal Alberti's desk. Fingering its half-inch thickness, the cleric preferred to read its executive summary first, before diving into the details.

FOUR ALBANIAN BURIAL
MOUND SUBJECTS.
EXECUTIVE SUMMARY

20.15.2018

CONDUCTED BY:
L.L GIFFON, A.M. ADAMS,
C.V. LUCCI , B.L. SULLIVAN

On 12.7.2018, Dr. G. Largo of the University of

Rome harvested, transported, and delivered to the forensic staff of the Vatican Gregorian Museum four individuals found on and within an Albanian burial mound of suspected Iron Age date (Plates 1-3, 12, 16, 25, 28-31, 34-40).

These remains consisted of one full human and three non-humans.

Human Remains (*Homo sapiens*)

The human, a male, had its throat completely severed as evidenced by a single, deep incision across the body of the C5 cervical vertebra (Plate 30). The location of the victim, found *in situ* behind the tomb's entranceway (Plates 28-29), supports the interpretation of a ritualized kill. There was considerable *post-mortem* evidence of predation to the head, hands and feet. The predation was committed by vermin infestation, specifically *Spalax graecus*, a local mole rat. This we know on the basis of numerous skeletal remains found throughout the burial. Dr. G. Largo provided ninety-three specimens.

Assignment: The subject was 153 centimeters tall. On the basis of its cranial measurements, the subject is classified as central European.

Overall Interpretation: Ritual murder or sacrifice.

Non-Human Remains
The three non-human subjects were taxonomically of two types.

Homo lupus

Two non-human males were found *in situ* atop the mound site within separate stone cist graves. The general skeletal remains were unremarkable. However, their dentition (Plates 34 a-b) evinced large upper and lower canines in excess of four centimeters. Their cranial orbits contained silver coins (dated to the sixth century AD) that fused themselves into the bone of the orbits' anterior chamber (Plates 35 a-b). The distal phalanges on both subjects displayed considerable abrasion, which was displayed as grooves on the inner surface of the stone slabs of the cist graves.

Heavy scoring (Plates 36 a-b) of these interior stone surfaces provide evidence that both subjects were buried alive.

Assignment: The subjects were 167 and 170 centimeters tall. Their overall skeletal classification suggests affinities to the ancient populations of the Ural Mountains. Kurgan?

Overall interpretation: The subjects were tortured and buried alive.

Mortuum bibet sanguine

The third non-human subject was found *in situ* within the mound's burial chamber. Stretched out in five directions, the subject was secured to the bedrock with heavy iron stakes with rings and heavy rope attached to silver shackles. The head was immobilized in a leather halter, while a silver bit locked the mandible open.

The condition of the subject's body was variable.

The axial skeleton and its soft tissues were generally intact, although heavily-desiccated, with signs of rodent predation to the ears, face, and torso. This subject's cranial orbits contained silver coins (dated to the early second century AD) that fused themselves into the bone of the orbits' anterior chamber. Further, the subject's dentition evinced massive upper canines in excess of 4 centimeters. The silver bit of the leather halter had fused into the upper and lower mandible at the coronoid process.

The subject's appendicular skeleton was found with clear, deep cutting or sawing marks on all the long bones. The silver manacles affixed to the wrists and ankles fused with the adjacent boney material.

Assignment: The subject was approximately 212 centimeters tall. The subject's overall skeletal type was classified as northern European.

Overall interpretation: a defleshing torture/sacrifice *in vivo*, followed by *post-mortem* vermin predation. Photographic imagery was not available.

Upon finishing the forensic report, the cardinal shuddered. After some consideration, he tapped an order into his laptop. The skeletal material was to be utterly incinerated. The resultant ash the laboratory technicians would mix with holy water into a thick slurry and then incorporate into the next cement repairs scheduled for the Vatican's streets.

Returning briefly to the report, the cleric flipped several pages and realized that the numismatic evidence proved the intrusive burials were not contemporaneous. While the burial of the tall vampire and the sacrificed human fell to the early second century, the two cist grave burials were nearly four centuries older. That troubled Alberti, as the ancients apparently used the mound twice as a place to bury their damned.

CHAPTER 7

The cardinal's interdepartmental memo about the destruction of the remains of the four individuals drew the collective frowns of the forensic team. Typically, the Vatican saved such unique evidence for any potential future investigations. It was not every day that the skeletons of two werewolves and the partial body of a vampire graced their extraordinary collection, which, among other things, included no less than four examples of the Yeti genotype.

Dr. Giffon, the team's French-speaking Swiss lead, groused at the cardinal's memo and then shrugged his shoulders. "In truth, we already have several similar specimens within the archive, but none of them—and I just checked, are in such good condition." Another Gallic shrug, "But orders are orders. Sullivan, take the remains to the crematory for destruction."

"Yes, doctor," the disappointed laboratory technician said. "It's a real shame. Their preservation is extraordinary."

"Noted Brian. But orders are orders," Giffon repeated.

And with that Brian Loomis Sullivan, an Irish Roman Catholic from Dublin, reached for a pair of latex gloves and stuffed them into his white lab coat pocket. On his way out of the laboratory's examination room, the lab tech took an examination cart.

The forensic team had temporarily stored the Albanian remains in the archaeological storage racking of the Gregorian Museum's basement level. The walk was not far. The building that housed the crematorium's furnace was conveniently nearby as well.

* * *

The vampire was once again self-aware in a vague and dreamy way. While it had sensed the warmth of the bright laboratory lighting, it had not felt the gathering of the various DNA and other tissue samples. The effects of the life-giving counter spell cast by Sister Gabriella had been far more pervasive than intended. Weak and debilitated far beyond human imagination, it lay in its body bag inert, somehow waiting at some primal level for an opportunity for nourishment.

* * *

Sullivan turned on the white porcelain wall switch and the basement section under its control illuminated in a soft golden yellow from pre-war light bulbs. The aisles that coursed between the massive building supports and shelving barely allowed the passage of the broad examination cart. Bumping the cart along, Sullivan accidently banged his right forearm on a sharp edge. Blood slowly began to weep. Letting out a choice Irish curse for his clumsiness, Sullivan hurried on, but now kept his arms well inside the cart's railing.

It was a good thing he knew where he was going in this underground labyrinth. Jokes abounded about getting lost amid all the shelving, dusty artifacts, and boxes with their cryptic labeling. Passing by one favorite:

1905.6.10 SUMERIA
Enlil Tempio
Strati 17.4.53, Vol. III, p. 33, P. 19-20
Figura pornografica

Sullivan chuckled to himself, "Someday, I have to open that one and take a peek."

Reaching the appropriate shelving location, Sullivan quietly swore under his breath that the four body bags he was looking for had been placed among several others from other excavations. To make matters worse, the bags' identifying labels were placed inside them to prevent their loss and to remove any possibility of their confusion.

Fortunately for Sullivan these ancient remains had

long ago gassed out. He zippered open the first, peered inside at its boney contents, and rummaged around for its label. It said:

> 1913.3.3 Babylon
> Grab 6
> Strate 9
> weiblicher Körper

"Nope, not that one."

Bag number two was one of the Albanian werewolves so he removed it, and placed it on the cart. Bag number three turned out to be the murdered Albanian human, and it too went on the cart. Bag number four, much fuller than the rest, was the tall Albanian vampire, but Sullivan had to make sure. He groped deeply into the bag for its identification tag. Unfortunately for Sullivan, his injured right forearm brushed against an enlarged canine leaving a bloody smear.

Chapter 8

Reflexively striking with the speed of a cobra, the vampire's mandibles clamped down on the laboratory technician's exposed forearm as it searched for an identification tag. Its two canines bit deeply. Blood spurted from a severed artery into the bag. Its mere smell was electric. Its taste orgasmic. The jaws would not let go. A long dormant tongue eagerly lapped at the hot, delicious, liquid.

*   *   *

At first Sullivan did not realize what had happened. He ignored the initial prick on his well-muscled arm. Past experience with countless sharp instruments, rugby injuries, and just as many scars, were a testimony to the Irishman's habitual clumsiness. But upon finding the tag, Sullivan tried to remove his arm from the bag and found that he could not. He jerked his arm twice, the bite wounds widened, the vampire's jaws sawed, and the former rugby player's' head went woozy. His knees failed. Slumping to the basement flooring his arm still firmly held in the bag, he collapsed, dragging the open bag down on top of him.

*   *   *

In all, the fit Irishman had carried over ten pints of blood in his system. Sigmund removed every bit of it to the point of collapsing the man's arterial system. Now capable of tentative movement, the blind vampire needed much more blood to fully reconstitute his form and sight. Before crawling away to hide in ambush for another victim, the vampire tore out the laboratory technician's livers and gorged upon them. Painful spasms of regrowth racked Sigmund's awakening conscience.

*   *   *

Several hours after Sullivan had been dispatched to the archaeological storage area, the incinerator foreman called up Dr. Giffon to ask when he might expect the materials scheduled to be burned on his work order.

Giffon blinked in confusion at the foreman's call. "I can assure you that I will look into this immediately. Thank you for your call."

"Who was that?" Adela Adams asked from behind her microscope while adjusting its focus.

"*Signore* Gappos. It seems that Sullivan has not made his delivery to the incinerator as yet."

Now glancing at her watch, "How is that possible? Brian may be a real klutz, but he is anything but late for anything."

"I agree." The laboratory supervisor said as he dialed up Sullivan's device and received no answer. Undeterred, he tried several more times and received the same result. "Adela, would you mind checking up on him? Perhaps retrace his steps? He is not answering his phone."

"Not a problem. Besides, my eyes could use a rest. Let *Signore* Gappos know to expect us shortly."

"Bless you, Adela."

Adams dark-brown hair bounced on her shoulders as she left the laboratory. A committed jogger since her days at Princeton, the youngish-looking woman was a serious go-getter with a brilliant and analytical mind. Armed with her microscope, the native of Denver, Colorado, allowed little to get past her.

Ever logical, Adams thought it best to go first to the archaeological storage area in the basement. She knew where she was going as both she and Sullivan had deposited the remains together in that basement's insane maze.

When Adams arrived she found the aisle lights on, shining their dull yellow. "Huh," she allowed while briskly continuing on. Upon turning onto the appropriate aisle, she saw several things ahead—the laboratory's cart with several items on it, and Sullivan face down on the floor. His lower back had been torn asunder.

"Oh, shit!" Adams blurted out as she sprinted the last few meters to her fallen colleague. Reaching him, she got down on one knee and turned him over. Immediately, she saw the ghastly pale complexion, vacantly dilated open eyes, a ragged wound on his right forearm, and total absence of blood. Then Adams heard a soft rustling off to her right.

* * *

With the second feast ingested, this time a female, Sigmund's eyes had regenerated to the point of blurry, but passable vision. While still weak and depleted by vampiric standards, the monster could now easily walk. Thoughts of escape from wherever he was, now entertained his mind. But first he would need clothing to do so. Standing upright for the first time in centuries, if not millennia, caused the being to stagger and in the process, Sigmund knocked over several items from the neighboring shelving with a noisy clatter, followed by the shattering of ceramics precious beyond words.

* * *

After an hour had passed, Giffon looked up from his paperwork and frowned. *Now where are Adams and Sullivan? They should be back by now from the incinerator.* Without hesitation he called Adams—again no answer. So he called Sullivan and received the same result. *Just what is going on here?* That was when he made a call to security.

"*Ciao. Sicurezza.*"

"Ah, yes, this is Dr. Giffon at the forensic laboratory.

"*Ah sì, Professore* Giffon, how may I be of service?"

"Officer, I am missing two of my laboratory technicians. Neither one is answering their phones. Both I sent to the archaeological storage area in the Gregorian Museum's basement. Could your department please look into their whereabouts?"

"*Assoultamente professore.* I will send two security guards immediately."

* * *

Five minutes later, the security guards found a horrific scene in the museum's basement. The two laboratory technicians were dead. Their bodies had been ripped open along their lower backs leaving large gaps where there should not have been any. Yet no blood could be found except here and there on the victims' clothing. And speaking of clothing, both victims were missing some—the male, his pants; the woman, her white lab coat.

* * *

Still quite emaciated, the vampire barely fit into the man's slacks, while he wore the white lab coat like a blousy dress shirt with several inches of exposed wrist sticking out of the sleeves. With partially matted black hair, a grayish skin tone, and a geeky, gaunt look, Sigmund made his escape from the museum's basement by following the posted red EXIT signs, correctly understanding their meaning as an abbreviation of the Latin word—*exitus*.

CHAPTER 9

Exiting from the bowels of the Gregorian Museum's basement, Sigmund, dressed like a later-day punk rocker in his tight slacks and strangely fitting white lab coat, was greeted by a warm fall evening. He was overcome with the scents of Rome—the heady perfume of blooming flowers, pine trees, errant sewer effluvia, and grilled garlic and onions.

With long shadows everywhere, the vampire stayed within them, following wall traces while seeking his way out of the densely built-up area. Along the way he encountered few pedestrians within this claustrophobic maze. Soon he encountered a high wall built of stone in various styles. He tried to follow its course looking for a gate, looking for his freedom, but was prevented by an imposing structure called the *Musei Vaticani*. He tentatively entered the imposing edifice through a side door entrance, flitted silently on his bare feet past the museum guards, and from a distance, shadowed a group of eleven tourists who seemed to know where they were going. In moments Sigmund found himself passing under a massive arch of white stone decorated with three monumental figures. More importantly, he was now out in the open and beyond the imposing high walls. Since the sun had set, the monster broke into a jog as he started across the piazza. Halfway, he broke into a dead run headed for the entrance of a crowded street and disappeared.

He now knew where he was—Rome—the city of the *Consilium*. That was the only possibility, given the Latin-based language, the old buildings, and the many inscriptions and monuments.

His problem: he did not know just when, as Arabic numerals made no sense to him. Despite that minor issue, more than hunger motivated him now, but the heady heat for revenge as well.

* * *

Sigmund instinctively headed north toward the suburb of CMES' international headquarters. As he did so passersby and those seated outdoor cafés sipping their evening red wine noted his passing. Some remarked that the bare-chested man looked to be a Croatian basketball player. Others, focusing upon his long curly hair and chiseled visage, speculated he was a movie star and this was some sort of a publicity stunt. The fact that he jogged and weaved through the crowds without being chased by the *polizia,* only meant the vampire's passage had been an oddity, one easily forgotten.

*   *   *

The day had ended with a macabre twist. Cardinal Alberti wound, and rewound the external security video for the fourth time of a pair of pants and a white lab coat that jogged away from the *Musei Vaticani*'s entrance facing the Viale Vaticano. The video was destined to be historic, for never before had such a poorly photogenic and completely soulless archaeological acquisition gotten up and run away from a museum's collection.

After a quick inventory check only the vampire's remains were found missing, as were a man's pair of pants and a white lab coat, confirming the video. As a precaution, the cardinal temporarily moved the two Albanian werewolves and the sole human remains to a more secure location within the museum. This entire train of thought was broken by a chime on his laptop.

"Ah, yes, Dr. Giffon. You are right on time," the cardinal murmured to himself.

After acknowledging his receptionist Father Joseph's message, the cleric waited for a beat, and he heard a door knock.

"Entrare."

"Bienvenue, Dr. Giffon. Thank you for coming so swiftly."

"*Mon plaisir*, Your Eminence," said the bedraggled forensic's director.

"When might I expect your second forensic report?"

"Perhaps tomorrow, Your Eminence, but before I write it, I wish to discuss the entire matter with you."

"Please do."

"Your Eminence, as you can probably imagine, it has been a very difficult day. On the one hand I have lost two of my laboratory technicians. And now, I have just performed their autopsies." The Frenchman sighed as tears formed in the corners of his blood-shot eyes.

"What did you find Dr. Giffon?"

"Too much, Your Eminence, too much. I suspect the initial attack on Sullivan was the result of his proverbial clumsiness. He had apparently scuffed his right forearm, blooding it. That somehow, someway set off the vampire's attack. Thereafter, Adela was simply ambushed."

The man paused, blew his long Gallic nose into his handkerchief, and continued.

"But I did discover something fascinating by total accident. The fact of the matter is that we do not understand vampire physiology very well. Intact ones are extremely hard to come by. While swabbing Brian's and Adela's wounds, I gathered a considerable amount of the vampire's saliva.

"Dr. Carlo Lucci of my team, per our usual procedure, ran an analysis of it and discovered an extremely poisonous protein mixed into the mucus. Cardinal Alberti, the poison was a neurotoxin most closely related to several infamous Amazonian spiders. When bitten, the neurotoxic reaction among humans can be easily mistaken for a common shock reaction, accompanied with generalized numbness, followed by heart failure. We surmise—in Sullivan's unfortunate case—that even while extremely desiccated, the vampire's teeth must have been coated with this highly-dangerous protein.

The forensic director stopped briefly to collect himself.

"The reason for this poisonous venom appears obvious—to enable the vampire to subdue its victim as quickly as possible. Apparently, a vampire cannot feed if its prey fights back."

"I see," the cleric said, "Now what about the remains of Drs. Sullivan and Adams? Should they be cremated?"

"Yes, immediately," the forensic director said sadly.

"Please Dr. Giffon, personally attend to their remains. Also include the two Albanian werewolf skeletons and the human sacrificial victim. Meanwhile, I will call *Signore* Gappos. I will also arrange for two security guards to accompany you."

"*Merci* Your Eminence."

After the door closed behind Giffon, the cardinal leaned forward against his desk and held his head in his hands. He began to shake. Tears darkened his desk's fiber blotter. After several moments, the red-eyed cleric's head rose as he spoke to the ceiling. "I sent Reissen to investigate and then Largo to collect those accursed remains. Sullivan and Adams were innocents. How many more will fall to this monster before we track it down?"

*   *   *

That first evening Sigmund fed, four times. But unlike his undisciplined days, he did so with extreme discretion and care. The four victims were impoverished street dwellers who were quietly taken in some of the darker habitation zones. Once finished, the monster deposited their remains into the sewer, which contained feral cats instead of rats. At his approach, they had scattered. Once satisfied, the monster took cover in one victim's shelter to hide in during the daylight hours. Along the way he pieced together his wardrobe from others' discards. Still quite problematic were shoes. In the end he reverted back to simple leather sandals.

The next evening, Sigmund moved on deeper into the northern suburbs of The Eternal City in search of the *Consilium*'s villa, found it, and marveled from afar at its constancy. Only the addition of odd protuberances along its roofline marred the pristine condition of the Roman villa's architecture. But at the mere sight of the hilltop structure the vampire erupted with waves of extremely violent emotion.

From his concealment deep within a pine grove, Sigmund was presented with an opportunity for revenge, as a member approached the villa. Vampiric eyes can see an individual's aura, and on that basis, can easily assess a potential victim's strength and abilities. What Sigmund saw was a powerful sensitive. Without another thought, he pounced and gorged himself. To his surprise, the victim's blood invigorated the vampire in ways that a human's could not. Warmth flowed through him, his skin took on a golden healthy glow, and his hair grew longer, shinier, and more luxuriant. Fully collapsing the victim's arterial system, he then tore out the livers and devoured them with relish. Unlike with the others, the monster did not dispose of the ragged mess, but instead brazenly dragged and deposited it on the very steps of the villa, much like a cat would present a dead mouse to its owner.

And so began Sigmund's personal war of revenge.

CHAPTER 10

While she had lived for a very long time, Astra—now known as Dannica—"Morning Star" in Danish, was also known by many other names. Adopting one was like trying on an article of clothing—something easily worn and then discarded when its appeal dimmed, its whimsy faded, or as necessity arose. As a consequence, any attempt to trace the vampire hunter's history was doomed to failure.

At her very core, Dannica dreaded the time when she would eventually run into her monster "father." This fixation went way beyond Carl Jung's well-known Electra Complex. For Dannica's very nature was anathema to her father's existence. Her entire life had been devoted to the hunt of fiends and the satisfaction of their kills.

Yet, despite all her experience and training, the dhampirica did not know how powerful her father was. Anything, she reasoned, that had lived so long, did so for a reason—its ability to survive and adapt. Dannica herself had experienced this process in action during her own long existence—some twenty-two hundred years, give or take.

Taking that personal experience as a rough

measure, the monster-killer inwardly shuddered. Yet, her ardent desire to kill Sigmund stemmed from the fact that he had created her—a hybrid human-vampire, who did not belong in the paranormal or mortal worlds. As if that were not sufficient motive, all Dannica had to do was think about her mother, Rovena, who had been forced to abandon her before succumbing to the vampire's poisonous infection. Either way, the monster deserved destruction.

*   *   *

For long-lived Dannica, with the prospect of simple companionship so rare, the successful formation of a true friendship was precious beyond words. That was exactly what Hidden Folk member and elder witch Portia Le Fey had gifted Dannica.

Le Fey had befriended the wandering dhampirica who was a refugee from the chaos of the mid-sixth century Germanic invasions of Italy. After a long voyage to the west, Dannica arrived at late Roman Barcino—modern Barcelona. There she met Le Fey, who completely understood Dannica's situation having been raised as a foundling herself. Le Fey, in her own way, became an older sister to Dannica, who improved her latent psychic abilities to include the reading of auras and telepathy. Also Le Fey offered the relative youngster much-needed social contact following the fall of the Etruscan Veca temple community to the onrushing forces of Christianity. Because of Le Fey, Dannica became a fringe associate of the Barcelona coven.

Dannica's relations with the Barcelona coven, while grudgingly acknowledged, had always been conducted at arm's length. While shunned by the coven's Hidden Folk, she nonetheless stalked monsters in the Catalan region in quiet anonymity just as she had in northern Italy. This last was the principle reason why the Hidden Folk had rejected her many overtures for membership within the Barcelona clan, as many within its ranks were in fact her prey of choice. As a consequence, her name never appeared on any coven roll or document; never appeared in any tale.

*　　*　　*

By the twenty-first century, Dannica wore her father's black hair long and straight, which framed her prominent Roman nose and large dark eyes perhaps a bit too harshly. She clothed her tall and taunt body with styles that were often torn, tattered, and care-worn—just like her.

Some frankly found her "look" at best artistically intriguing, at worse, the gaunt shade of a Nazi concentration camp inmate. Dannica's diet of fresh livers had staved off aging, heightened the woman's five senses, preserved her finely-textured skin, and if allowed to gorge, built muscle mass. Oddly, she threw little shadow. Above all, hunting monsters remained her sport of choice and she was *damn* good at it.

*   *   *

On that fateful day when a sniper claimed the witch and elder Portia Le Fey on her balcony, Dannica had been sunning below in the cathedral's sunny courtyard. Hiding behind a pair of Ray Ban sunglasses, she blended seamlessly amid the tourists, wearing a pair of stylishly torn jeans and a faded AC/DC tee shirt.

At the repetitive mechanical coughing sounds of the sniper's rifle, her hunter's senses went on high alert. Tasting the air and scenting fresh blood, her mouth reflexively watered. While Dannica heard the direction of the attack, she had difficulty locating the source in the bright morning sunlight. Finally, she located it.

Somewhere over there, and high above from a rooftop, she judged.

Next, what stood out to Dannica, was a willowy

woman of medium height wearing a wide straw hat and billowing turquoise-colored sundress. Her body language screamed nervous energy and purpose, as she got up from her place in a nearby café. Her aura said the same. Most damning, Dannica could sense the woman's irritation as her morning cappuccino was only half-finished.

But the ultimate confirmation of her suspicions came when the woman in turquoise strode over to the arched portico of the fallen elder's apartment. She carried only a white plastic grocery bag and no handbag. That detail jolted Dannica's attention. But there was something else about the woman, something special that marked her as noteworthy. Her mind was completely blocked from telepathic intrusion.

She's an adept!

Recognizing this, Dannica casually got up from her place in the sun, stretched like an uninterested feline, and sauntered over to a position to watch and see what might happen next.

Seven minutes later, the woman in turquoise reappeared from the flat's portico, with that walk of purpose again. At the nearest trash bin, she deposited the white plastic bag, its contents, and her expensive sunhat. Her now free-flowing black hair blew in the breeze as she walked down a narrow side passage and away from the cathedral's courtyard.

Now more than curious, Dannica risked hurrying to her friend's flat, knocked, received no reply, and used her personal key. Only then did she understand—the woman was part of the murder team. She had sterilized Le Fey's torn and destroyed form with blessed salt, thus preventing any chance of her resurrection through Hidden Folk means. That detail alone told Dannica the woman was a witch who must be found and questioned. Once that was accomplished, the identity of the true murderer would surely follow. The monster hunter was sure of it.

Dannica stood over the fallen form of her dear friend and confidant, which lay in an expanding pool of blood—entirely covered in a thick layer of salt. It took all of her control not to bend over and clutch her friend to her breast and grieve. Instead, her face hardened.

Lo' unto them! For my vengeance will be the thing of nightmare.

Upon returning to street level, Dannica walked over to the trash bin, retrieved the plastic bag, and inspected its contents. She found three empty cylinders of blessed salt and a pair of wooden-soled sandals marred with flecks of her friend's blood and embedded grains of salt. The wooden-soled sandals only further confirmed that the woman in the sundress was an outright witch. The sandals would have insulated the woman from any of Le Fey's passive defensive magic.

Next, Dannica retrieved the discarded sunhat. Holding it close, the monster hunter breathed deeply and fully scented the woman's perfume down to her shampoo. One item stuck out—the heady smell of the lotus blossom. *She's probably Egyptian*, Dannica surmised. *That would match her appearance quite well and the choice of her dress color.*

Returning the sunhat to the bin, Dannica breathed in the air as she walked in the direction taken by the retreating woman in the turquoise sundress. As she followed her quarry's scent, her mind churned.

She looks Egyptian, smells Egyptian, and even wears the lucky blue color of an Egyptian. That makes her Egyptian. How interesting ...

Arriving at the next intersection, Dannica looked around and in the distance saw the woman waiting at a curbside. Fearlessly she continued and closed within twenty meters of her quarry, unsure of what to do given it was broad daylight. Then, a plain, white paneled van pulled over. Its gaping side door opened revealing it also contained several pieces of luggage, and the woman in turquoise disappeared. As the vehicle pulled away, Dannica memorized its license plate number.

Interesting. This was a well-planned murder from start to finish. They are probably headed for the airport now to make their getaway. Cairo perhaps?

One block away from where the woman in turquoise got into the panel van, Dannica sprinted to the underground metro system and linked a series of trains to the Barcelona International airport. It took her close to forty minutes to arrive and Dannica knew her quarry had arrived ahead of her, still. The monster hunter hoped to pick up her distinctive scent.

Once in the main terminal, Dannica walked its length tasting the air. Near the women's bathroom, her sensitive nose snagged something and she entered. In one of the facility's rear trash bins, Dannica found the woman's discarded blue sundress. Reaching in, the hunter buried her face in its cloth and took a deep breath. Her senses now imprinted with her quarry's complete range of smells, she left the bathroom. Dannica again scented the air, picked up a fading trail, and followed it unquestioningly.

Dannica descended a staircase that led to a corridor, which she followed. After about a hundred yards, she found herself entering the private commuter terminal side of the airport. Here the scent gained considerably in strength. Passing by several unattended check-in counters, Dannica stopped at the fourth that was occupied. Approaching the young uniformed attendant with a broad smile, the monster hunter inquired about her friend—a stunningly beautiful woman with raven black hair. During the inquiry, Dannica lightly hypnotized the gate attendant while implanting the woman's scent in his mind.

Seeing the attendant's eyes slightly dilate at the scent's recognition, Dannica found out the destination of the passenger—the United States and not Egypt. This was a surprise. The passenger's name soon followed unbidden. "Dr. Melaina Makris."

"Could you kindly tell me which airport in the States is her destination?"

"Latrobe," came the easy reply. Confused by the sound of the destination, Dannica reached over to shake the man's hand, thanking him. At her touch she whispered, "Forget," and walked away leaving the man to return to several mundane tasks.

As Dannica strode away from the counter, her mind was running at a mile-a-minute.

Alright, this witch-woman, adept, whatever, is Dr. Melaina Makris. What kind of witch is that? Her name is Coptic Greek in origin and not Islamic, so she still could be Egyptian, yet she is flying on a private jet to the US. That alone suggests either expensive tastes or considerable financial resources. More importantly, she broke into Portia's flat—no mean feat given all of her defensive wards. That screams "adept." But this Dr. Makris is not even Portia's murderer, she just finished up the job. That makes her only a part of something far larger.

Finally,

Who are these people? And where is Latrobe?

*   *   *

Having returned to her apartment by metro, Dannica searched online and found out "Latrobe" was a regional airport in western Pennsylvania. She blinked hard as that region tickled her memory.

So who within the paranormal community has the resources for a private jet? Both CMES and ... TIIIS. Since the jet was headed for the US, probably not CMES. That leaves ... TIIIS ... The International Integrated Interface Society! What a weird name, she randomly thought.

After a quick Google Earth search, *Yes! Now I remember! TIIIS' US training facilities are only some*

twenty minutes drive away from Latrobe! It was TIIIS'
Lictor of Magic who was the champion of the Contest in
the Alakrum Desert!

Again thinking rapidly, *the destruction of the*
Barcelona coven occurred shortly after that contest. In
fact, I distinctly remember hearing about several other
unsolved assassinations that took place throughout
eastern and central Europe during that time.

The monster hunter's working hypothesis soon
became—*TIIIS probably took out the Barcelona coven*
as part of a whirlwind pass across the continent
following the contest. That made Portia's murder a
clean-up job—the completion of the extermination of
the Barcelona coven's members.

Those bastards! That makes Dr. Makris a member
of TIIIS and in league with its Lictor of Magic.

*　　*　　*

Dannica sat back deep in her chair. The sheer act of that
grand coven's massacre, and now the balcony
assassination of her close friend, shocked her. The
revelation that she now had a lead on who did it
brought hope, but also made her blood boil. The heat of
anger and the overpowering desire for vengeance over
what she considered a personal assault flowed through

her veins like molten metal. For the first time in a long time, Dannica contemplated a grand adventure, a quest for pure revenge, and the dhampirica welcomed it.

CHAPTER 11

Dannica's quest for revenge, however, was temporarily blunted by the gruesome and graphic archaeological news out of Albania. As with all such things that jolt the system by sheer accident, Dannica was made aware of the Albanian excavation from the Catalan newspaper *El Punt Avui*. There, splashed across the front-page upper fold, was a leaked photo of the mound's central burial. No half-decomposed skeleton appeared, just five iron-ringed stakes in the shape of a pentagram hammered into the bedrock, followed by lurid commentary filled with unsupportable suppositions and impossibly gossamer associations.

Many underground communities and public paranormal societies of Europe were entranced by the article's implications, and some, notably those at CMES-Rome, were quite embarrassed by the exposé, for they knew precisely what it represented and why. Meanwhile, Dannica's interest was piqued because she knew what it signified as well—a brutal execution, one that her own Etruscan religious order had occasionally undertaken. She found herself asking, *Could this possibly be my father's burial?*

The fallout however, did not end there. The article

went on to list the participation of the Vatican, and specifically the Gregorian Museum, and one of its representatives, Dr. Erik Reissen, in the burial mound's investigation. Such unwanted publicity sent a shockwave through the Holy See, and the Pro Deo community in particular.

Although not specifically mentioned by name, Cardinal Alberti, as the operational director of Pro Deo, hit the roof over the flap. He absolutely forbade the photogenic and well-known Egyptologist Reissen from meeting with the press. In addition, the cleric dressed down the Austrian for not providing sufficient security on the excavation's photographic imagery, and even challenged his credentials for not having removed the five ringed stakes from the burial's bedrock. To add salt to the wound, the excavations' field photographer, Geoffrey Smith, was nowhere to be found.

"Your Eminence," Reissen began as he stood at attention with his hands behind his back before the cleric's desk, "I do not believe that our field photographer was the source of this image or the information so scandalously portrayed in the newspaper article."

"Explain yourself, Dr. Reissen," the cardinal tersely challenged.

"The photo that appeared in the newspaper is missing an important detail."

"Such as?" the cardinal bridled.

"The image did not contain any of the restraining ropes, their silver manacles, or the head-halter."

"And that observation is supposed to take away my migraine? Perhaps cure my ulcer?" the cleric popped an antacid tablet into his mouth.

"No, Your Eminence. But given the politics at the Albanian university, I suspect an insider took this photo in order to embarrass someone. This exposure is meant to be used as leverage for some purpose. Also remember the Moslem component in this matter. Any taint of magic is totally taboo in their religion, while simultaneously enflaming local superstitions. The mention of the Vatican, our museum, and myself, only adds fuel to their internecine politics. In the end with them it is all about who controls the funding."

"Are you suggesting that we should shut down the cultural exchange?"

"No Your Eminence," the Austrian said with a shake of his head, "We should stay the course and ride this out."

"Dr. Reissen, you had better be right on this."

"I hope I am too Your Eminence."

"Now what about your field photographer? What happened to Smith?"

"Geoffrey is keeping a low profile, Your Eminence. In fact, I have just spoken with him, and frankly, he is quite frightened by all the press."

"Do you believe him?" the cleric asked pointedly.

"Yes Your Eminence, I do. Geoffrey is a good man who finds himself in a tight situation."

"We all are, Dr. Reissen. We all are."

At this point in the meeting, Reissen thought that it was over and was about to turn to leave, but the cleric paused, and then tapped on his laptop.

He spun the device around on his desk blotter, "Dr. Reissen, I want you to see this security video. Tell me what you see."

After a few moments, "Has this been photoshopped? A pair of pants and a white lab coat jogging? Is this some kind of joke? If it is, I am missing the point."

"Dr. Reissen, what you are looking at is all that a security video camera could capture of an escaping vampire, the very same one that Dr. Largo brought back from Albania."

"What?"

"Yes, and yesterday two of our own forensic

laboratory technicians became its prey."

The Austrian's back stiffened as his face turned white at the news. "That explains all the recent high security."

"Yes, Dr. Reissen, it surely does."

*   *   *

Once Reissen had left the cleric's office, an idea came to Alberti. He briefly studied his wristwatch, smiled, and made a transatlantic call on his personal device, instead of using the Vatican's landline.

"President Silver Moon," the woman said.

"*Presidente* Silver Moon, this is Cardinal Alberti in Rome. How are you on this fine morning?"

"Cardinal Alberti! What a surprise. And how did you know ... well ... of course you knew." The woman bubbled with warmth as brilliant sunshine poured into her Santa Fe office. Then the president of TIIIS shifted gears and got down to business. "What can I do for you, Your Eminence?"

"*Madam Presidente*, there is a vampire abroad in Rome. It has already claimed two of my people, and I fear other innocents will fall as well. Is your Lictor of Magic available?"

Silver Moon paused to consider the request, which

she was more than happy to honor, but she had several questions that needed answering before she deployed J.J. Stone all the way to Rome.

"Cardinal Alberti," Silver Moon asked as delicately as she could, "I know the Vatican has resources that can handle a vampire. Are they not available?"

"*Madam Presidente,* sadly I cannot ask for their assistance as it was my department, Pro Deo, who has caused this situation in the first place."

"Could you perhaps explain that Cardinal Alberti?"

"Ah, yes. The vampire in question was recovered by my department, *Madam Presidente.*"

As Silver Moon listened to this thin and vague explanation, she realized that the man was trying to clean up a mess of his own creation. To ask another Vatican department to fix the issue could most likely lead to a politically volatile situation. In short, the cleric was in a serious bind. Silver Moon made a snap decision.

"When would you like our Lictor of Magic to arrive Your Eminence?"

*   *   *

Cardinal Alberti's private call was anything but. Receivers first intercepted it, then recorded, and passed on the information to be analyzed by a competing organization located in a northern suburb of Rome. While the cleric had managed to evade the Vatican's own landline security systems, CMES now knew about his predicament firsthand.

"Mr. Gnotti," the security technician said, "we just received a communication from Cardinal Guillermo Alberti, operations head of the Vatican's Pro Deo department."

"From where?" Gnotti asked.

"His personal device sir."

"Interesting. Apparently the cardinal does not even trust his own security apparatus. Send it over to me immediately," the director of Communications and Security for the CMES-Rome center said into his stalk microphone. He added, "Good work, and place a red flag on his device. I want to know anything else that he might want to say."

"Yes sir."

Moments later the man read, and then reread, the phone call's transcript. It was extremely rare that CMES was granted a peek into the Vatican's dirty laundry, and Gnotti was mesmerized by the quality of that filthy linen—a vampire on the loose in Rome and Alberti felt responsible for it. *How delicious.*

Then, Gnotti's mind began spinning. *Is this the same vampire that is plaguing us?* Then another thought came forth unbidden. *Or, is this vampire a Vatican weapon sent against us?*

Gnotti, quickly reached a decision. He picked up his phone and called his superior, Chairman DeSalvo. Of all the people in CMES-Rome, he would want to know about this development immediately.

CHAPTER 12

Dannica needed to talk to someone in-the-know about the newspaper's photograph. She had a million questions—most she could not ask directly, but could perhaps glean indirectly. So the next day she flew from Barcelona to Rome's Leonardo da Vinci Airport with the newspaper article in hand. Traveling light with only a small wheelie, she took a cab directly to The Fragrance Hotel St. Peter—a ten-minute walk from Vatican City. Her goal was simple—find and talk to Dr. Erik Reissen. Her pretext was equally simple—she was an Etruscan archaeologist who specialized in funerary architecture—a fact that she had indeed lived. She had even concocted a name for herself—Dr. Dannica Ruthmann.

To her surprise, navigating through the Gregorian Museum was relatively straightforward. Yes, the monster hunter had to pass through several metal detectors, but that was about it. Only once did she have to double-talk her way past a guard, stating that she had an appointment with the museum's librarian.

Dannica's search led her through the administrative floors, but eventually, she stood before a closed wooden office door. Next to it on the wall was a modest bronze plaque engraved with the words "Dr. E. G. Reissen." Brazenly, she knocked on the wooden door three times. From within she heard a surprised, "Herein bitte." With a simple turn of the bronze doorknob, the monster hunter stood face-to-face with the man she believed had found her father's tomb.

Reissen looked up from his desk, his eyebrows raised in surprise and bluntly asked, "Can I help you?"

"I am sorry to disturb you Dr. Reissen," Dannica passably said in the man's native German, "but I am Dr. Dannica Ruthmann of the Catholic University in Milano. I am an Etruscan archaeologist. My specialty is funerary architecture. I wish to talk to you about your recent work in Albania. Do you have a moment for a colleague?"

Reissen was dumbfounded on several levels. First, how did this woman get to his office given all the heightened security since the vampire's escape? Second, her striking and youthful appearance spelled trouble—anything but an academic colleague—maybe even a reporter in disguise—something that the cardinal had told him to avoid at all costs. And third, his sixth sense was absolutely screaming into his ear. Trapped as he was, ultimately the Austrian's inbred sense of hospitality overcame his wariness. Standing, the archaeologist gestured to the lone visitor's chair and said testing, "Please, Dr. Rutmann, take a seat."

"Thank you, Dr. Reissen, but my name is pronounced Ruthmann."

"Ah, my apologies, Dr. Ruthmann. What can I do for you?" the Austrian emphasized with two open hands.

Seated as demurely as she could in her black tube dress, Dannica began. "Most Etruscan tombs I have excavated are elaborately domed structures. May I ask, is that what you encountered in Albania?"

Reissen's sixth sense flared intensely again. He was suspicious and reticent to discuss any details about the Albanian excavation, especially over such a rudimentary question. So, he flat out stonewalled the woman.

"Frankly, Dr. Ruthmann, the person you should speak with is Professor Dr. Lorenc Galaty of the Albanian University in Tirana. He is in charge of the excavation. Would you like his contact information? I would be happy to provide it."

Dannica did not find Reissen the typical academic, ivory tower type. He was ruggedly handsome, tanned, and clearly fit. She liked his frank and direct demeanor, even if it was a helpful and outright rejection.

Reissen, on the other hand, was put off by the woman and her intrusion into his intellectual lair. But more than that, the archaeologist sensed her unstated thoughts, which held dark secrets and emotional pain. Clearly, at least in Reissen's mind, the woman was deeply troubled.

Meanwhile, sensing the impenetrable firmness of the archaeologist's mind, Dannica identified the man as either a latent sensitive or all-out professional. Either possibility made her heart skip a beat.

"Dr. Galaty's contact information would be much appreciated Dr. Reissen."

Tearing off a sheet of scrap paper the Austrian wrote down several lines from memory, passed it to Dannica, and stood, indicating the end of their conversation.

"Thank you, Dr. Reissen," Dannica said, first picking up the note and then extending her hand. The Austrian took it and blinked. Upon contact, Reissen received a violent psychic download of just who Dannica was and why she had searched him out. A pang of sympathy squeezed at his heart.

Dannica was totally unaware of this transference. Instead, she again expressed her gratefulness for him sharing the contact information and turned to leave.

Reissen then abruptly said, "Dr. Ruthmann, please accept my apologies, but I believe that I have forgotten my collegial manners. Please sit down," he added with an inviting gesture of his hand.

Surprised, but again hopeful, Dannica did so.

"Dr. Ruthmann, I think that we have much to discuss."

The monster hunter sat in silence, waiting. *What just happened? The man's demeanor has changed entirely.*

"Dr. Ruthmann … Dannica … or perhaps I should address you as … Astra," Reissen began.

Hearing her birth name being voiced, and after such a long time, shocked the monster hunter and she covered her mouth with her hand. *This man is an adept! He just read my mind somehow. Wait. I did feel an odd tingling sensation when we shook hands. That's how he did it!"*

"I am very sorry for what others have done to your father. But the terms 'justice' and 'vengeance' in the paranormal world too often blur together."

Dannica, speechless at the man's bluntness, could only stiffly nod in agreement, her face an emotionless surface.

"Dr. Ruthmann, you should know that we

recovered the remains of a very tall individual from that burial mound in Albania. The forensic department's report said it was not human. Unfortunately, the museum is no longer in possession of these remains for you to view. For that, I am sorry," the Austrian concluded with folded hands.

Finding her tongue, Dannica asked, "What happened to these remains?"

An odd smile crossed Reissen's face before he answered. He typed several strokes into his laptop, then, "Dr. Ruthmann. Take a look at this two-day-old security video and tell me what you see." He spun around his laptop's screen to face his visitor.

With eyes wide, Dannica whispered, "I see a running pair of pants and a white lab coat."

"Is that all?"

"Please replay the video."

After the second playing of the security video Dannica asked, "How?"

"Two of our forensic technicians were attacked in a storage area and killed. Apparently their blood and livers were sufficient for the vampire's revival. He is now on the loose in Rome."

"That's incredible."

"Yes, indeed it is. Do you know what the vampire

looks like? The forensic team measured him at 212 centimeters."

"Yes … my father is quite tall … I saw him last when he attacked my mother."

"Do you think you could pick him out in a crowd?" the Austrian asked.

"Definitely. I also know him by scent."

"I see." Reissen paused. "May I ask, how old are you, Dr. Ruthmann?"

The monster hunter turned her head slightly aside both to calculate the vast span of time and then translate it into a meaningful expression. "I think I was born sometime in the mid-second century BC."

Reissen somehow was not surprised by that answer, but instead said, "You have seen much, have you not?"

A nod, "Perhaps too much."

Then Reissen looked her straight in the eye and with a quiet voice full of steel said, "Dr. Ruthmann, you are a monster hunter. You walked into my office looking for evidence of your vampiric father, so you could rid yourself of him. Is that not so?"

A single slow nod.

"Alright. Now you know. He is Rome. Now do us all a favor, and do *your* job."

The two stood and shook hands again, this time without the intense psychic download. Dannica now held Reissen's contact information as he did hers.

"Stay in touch," the Austrian ordered.

"I will, and, thank you again."

As the woman left his office, Reissen noted that she had left behind the scrap of paper with Galaty's contact information.

*   *   *

As soon as his office door was closed, Reissen made a call.

"*Caio*, Cardinal Alberti's office." Father Joseph efficiently greeted.

"Father Joseph, this is Dr. Reissen, I need to speak with the cardinal immediately."

"Un momento, Profesore Reissen."

Moments later the cardinal greeted, "*Caio* Dr. Reissen."

"Your Eminence, I think that I have stumbled upon both an ally and a solution regarding that odd security video of yours."

"Explain."

"Your Eminence, the vampire's daughter, a dhampirica, just left my office."

"Sweet Jesus! What did you discuss?"

"All I told her was he was loose in Rome."

"This is *extraordinary* news Erik!"

"I thought that you would see it that way."

"What is she going to do?"

"Your Eminence, by definition she is a monster hunter. But she is also heavily conflicted as this particular monster is her father."

"Do you think she will follow through?"

"Unknown. We will have to be patient Your Eminence. But I would suggest that we have a backup plan ready to implement."

"Agreed. And Erik …"

"Yes, Your Eminence …"

"Well done."

"Thank you Your Eminence."

The cardinal sat back in his chair and whispered to himself, "Now I have two solutions."

CHAPTER 13

Outsiders often believe that the paranormal world is one composed of stark contrasts and harshly defined opposites—good and bad. Nothing could be further from the truth. Nonetheless, this commonly held myth has as its origin the competition of two organizations that have dominated the paranormal scene for millennia.

By far, the oldest paranormal organization is the *Consilium magorum et sagarum*, or CMES. The "mother coven" was founded in the ancient Sumerian city of Ur sometime during the fourth millennium BC. After a horrific sacking of that city, the enclave moved to Egyptian Memphis during the second millennium BC. There it prospered until the capture of Egypt by Octavius' armies. Pragmatically seeing the writing on the wall, CMES resettled in Rome just before the birth of Christ, and has remained there until this very day. By its very nature, CMES is a pagan institution.

By the twentieth century, CMES had developed into an international organization with vast financial resources and tremendous clout. Its corporate tentacles reached nearly everywhere—even the US government had not been immune to its influence and corruption until the purge of twenty-two of its elected officials.

Standing in opposition to CMES was another paranormal organization, which is currently called *The International Integration and Interface Society*, or TIIIS. Unlike CMES, its name changed throughout the millennia because of its constant persecution and consequent need for anonymity.

Founded in Rome during the second century BC as a conservative reaction against the influx of human sacrifice, TIIIS initially co-existed with the elder coven. That is until CMES wrongfully made its existence known to the Imperial Roman administration and slandered it as a subversive organization. In many ways, TIIIS and Early Christianity were used as scapegoats to cover up CMES' infelicities and to protect its membership. This, therefore, is the source of both TIIIS' and the Roman Catholic Church's deep and abiding hatred for CMES, and the ultimate origin of the outsider view of a paranormal world made up of stark contrasts.

Further, due to this accident of TIIIS' initial association with Early Christianity, and the irony of its later persecution by Christianity itself, TIIIS evolved differently. Their associations of sensitives and paranormal adepts remained timidly in hiding just to survive—much like the early mammals of the later dinosaur periods. Only with the dawn of the European Enlightenment did TIIIS dare emerge into the light of day, and eventually established its international headquarters in the United States. It was only during the beginning of the twenty-first century that its Lictor of Magic challenged, and then humbled, the paranormal supremacy of the elder coven.

CMES' international headquarters were located at a villa that stood atop a hillock of limestone and barren, lifeless sand within an otherwise heavily-wooded Roman suburb. When seen from the air, its faded red-tiled roof surrounded a parched gravel and terrazzo enclosure with deeply-shadowed porticos. This desolate façade fronted a myriad of underground chambers that honeycombed the bedrock of this stoutly-defended outcrop. Stark and forbidding, this villa was reverently referred to by its membership as *Romae matrem*, "Mother Rome," since its relocation there in 30 BC.

*   *   *

Sigmund's first bloody predations against CMES, delivered to their very doorstep, had been thoroughly videotaped. The problem, however, was the same as with the Vatican's security cameras—Sigmund's image could not be captured—just his garments. When CMES' security personnel were dispatched, there was no one to apprehend. Instead, they could only retrieve the ravaged bodies of their membership. Thoroughly frustrated, they did not know who was doing it, much less why.

CMES' current international chairman, William DeSalvo, had risen through the ranks. Battle-hardened, the Roman chairman took the murders of his people as a personal affront and began knocking heads over why the imagery from their security cameras were so useless in identifying the culprit.

"*Signor Presidente*," the Director of Communications and Security at the Rome center said, "I have just been reminded that those without souls cannot be photographed or video-taped."

"Thank you for that nuanced tidbit of paranormal minutia, but where does that leave us, *Signore* Gnotti?"

"That our attacker is a vampire, *Signor Presidente*. Not only can we not produce an image of it, but its victims have been ravaged—and by that I mean totally exsanguinated and with their livers missing."

Thinking. the chairman tapped at his teeth with his forefinger, while seeking some tangible clue. Then, "Why now, *Signore* Gnotti?"

"*Signor Presidente*, I cannot assign a motive for these murders, just that this vampire wants us to know of them," the director of Communications and Security answered. "However, *Signor Presidente*, the Vatican *did* admit they lost a vampire."

The chairman's eyes made the connection and registered the fact. "What are the odds, *Signore* Gnotti, that the original incept was purposely misleading?"

"Very low *Signor Presidente*. Consider: why would the Vatican admit to such a thing?"

"Good point. Now who do we have available to take out this threat?"

"*Bona fide* monster hunters, dhampirs, the naturally-born ones, are extremely rare to come by. Certainly none are known of in Italy."

"What about champions? Can they be brought in to do the job?"

"I would not recommend it," Gnotti said with a shake of his head. "Our reputation with the use of champions after the Contest in the Alakrum Desert is still quite fresh among their community."

At this the chairman grunted in appreciation, but then asked, "You know of no vampire hunters *per se*?"

"*Signor Presidente*, such individuals are principally the fiction of Hollywood. But as during the last two days four of our local members have been murdered, I recommend that we inform them of the threat and to act accordingly."

"In other words, *Signore* Gnotti, you are telling me that we are powerless and being held hostage to a renegade vampire."

Gnotti remained mute. Meanwhile, DeSalvo yearned for the wisdom, experience, and creativity of his former armorer, Mitzi Randolph, a polite but otherwise ruthless shape-shifter.

"You are not willing to deploy our security force, are you?"

After a thoughtful moment, "To what purpose *Signor Presidente*? I must address the morale of our troops above all. If I send them out full in the knowledge that at least half of them will be expended in the exercise, is that the wisest use of them?"

"Alright, *Signore* Gnotti. What about battling a vampire with a vampire?"

"Now that is an interesting thought."

"*Signore* Gnotti, I am not interested in your opinion, I want results, NOW!"

"*Sì Signor Presidente.*"

*   *   *

Within the hour, Gnotti gathered for a meeting three vampires from the Rome membership. All had martial backgrounds.

"Thank you for agreeing to meet with me on such short notice. Our coven has a crisis that I am quite sure you are aware of. Four of our members have been brutally murdered and left quite literally on our doorstep. A vampire did this. I am asking each of you to assist in the defense of what is ours. Are you willing?"

The three vampires in the conference room, two females and a male, first looked at each other, and then as one, nodded their assent.

"Thank you. Here is what we know, which sadly, is not much."

*   *   *

After his four swift kills, Sigmund noticed the villa had gone quiet—no visitors, no deliveries. Yes, their security force had removed the remains of his latest meals and had expertly cleaned up his mess, but nothing other than that. From his hidden place of observation, the vampire rightly sensed the coming of *something*, some sort of response. This frankly, he warmly welcomed.

* * *

Typically vampire hunts are all about the scent of the prey. This Gnotti's three assigned hunters did not have, not directly, but all of Sigmund's victims carried his saliva. That would have to do, and after a fashion, the three "scented" Sigmund. In so doing, they pieced together much more about their quarry.

"Old, extremely old, is this one, even by my standards," dark-haired Carla offered. She was the eldest, a Renaissance-made vampire, who as a young mortal had often seen the master Michelangelo buying pigments in the Roman marketplace. She had been a rough and tough street urchin and deft pick-pocket when made a vampire.

"Male, it is male," Monica added with certainty—herself a creation of the chaos of the European Second World War. She had lived through Buchenwald, was a survivor, only to be made after her release by the Allies. She had been waylaid by a vampiric SS officer on his way to Argentina. Red-headed and gaunt, the Jewess had no patience for needless slaughter.

"I agree it is male, but it is not old, but ancient, as in millennia," added Bruno, a well-proportioned brute, and former Iron Curtain wrestler from the 1950's.

"Why ancient?" Carla asked.

"Because its scent reminds me of the graveyards I used to work in as a boy. Occasionally we would come across an ancient's plot while digging a fresh one."

"Ancient graves have a scent?" Monica challenged in total disbelief.

"Yes and no. But they often have a feeling about them that always seemed to tickle my nose."

"So," Carla unnecessarily summarized, "we have a potentially ancient male vampire to kill. Now, who wants to be the bait?"

So ended the planning session of three individuals who had never before worked together as a team.

* * *

To Sigmund's great pleasure, that evening the coven's response came in the form of three distinct scents—two females and a male—vampires all. This he easily divined since they were on the hunt. How? Because with all predatory creatures, the excitement of the chase caused shifts in bodily chemistry. He also knew they were not profession huntsmen, for if they were, they would have known how to hide such an obvious telltale.

Sigmund waited patiently within the boughs of a nearby pine grove. With his scent so masked, he waited like a spider at the edge of his web.

The first of his like to appear was a large hulking figure who cowered in the villa's doorway, looking this way and that—his nervous sweat apparent on the wind. This told Sigmund that he was only the opening act of some sort of ambush.

Then, in quick succession, two other scents reached his nostrils, both to his right. These others were on the move, apparently getting into a position from where the big one could be seen. Sigmund surmised they expected him to take the proffered bait, only then would they pounce. But the wily vampire had a better idea.

Reaching up to a convenient branch dripping with summer sap, Sigmund smeared himself with the sticky substance, except for around his nose. He began to slither his way out of the grove and into the tall ornamental grass, imagining himself a snake. Now peering between the tall stalks, he located the other two vampires. They were hiding behind a low stuccoed wall that separated properties. To him, the situation was almost comical. Now knowing where his ambushers were, he carefully backed up, and slithered on in another direction.

Given the size of Sigmund's hands and the narrowness of the two vampire's necks, he completed his stalk by simply reaching out and snapping them both from behind. For good measure, he stomped down and crushed both of their heads. While messy, the act also prevented any possibility of them catching up with him unawares. To make sure, he waited several minutes until the flesh of their bodies began to decompose, breaking down into fluffy motes that disappeared on the breeze.

As for the big one that still lurked near the villa's entrance, Sigmund just walked up the villa's circular driveway and brazenly dared it to engage him.

"You there. Witless one," Sigmund pointed and taunted in Latin. "I am here," he said expansively, with arms open in greeting. "Take me if you dare."

Bruno, who did not understand a word of the Latin challenge, understood the vampire's body language well enough, and charged recklessly headlong. Wishing to grapple with his tormentor, Sigmund denied the wrestler his wish by deftly stepping to one side while tearing out his throat. Throwing the still pulsing mass of flesh upon the villa's steps, he engaged the wounded vampire, broke his neck, and then crushed Bruno's head under his foot. As the vampire walked away from the villa, Bruno's flesh began to fall and drift away.

* * *

The first thing DeSalvo noticed when he reviewed the latest security video with Gnotti was the aggressor had taunted Bruno in Latin. Hearing it almost caused the chairman to laugh, if the situation had not been so dire. The swift dispatch of the three vampires said a lot. Clearly the vampire was formidable—if not ancient.

While he did not want to make a call for help, he also knew through hard experience that his pride would eventually heal. His coven came first.

"*Signore* Gnotti, I have seen enough. What is the condition of the other two?"

"Destroyed."

"I see *Signore* Gnotti. That is most unfortunate. Again inform the membership of the heightened danger and instruct them to not approach headquarters for any reason whatsoever. Maintain the villa under high alert, and make preparations for a possible hostile intruder."

"*Sì Signor Presidente.*"

When Gnotti left his cubical, DeSalvo turned to his laptop and made a Skype call. It was the one that he was looking forward to. It would be a test, for if the Vatican had really called TIIIS for help, then his request would reveal much. Before he stabbed the ENTER key to initiate it, he too made a quick mental calculation. Yes, it was now or never.

*   *   *

"Well hello there, Chairman DeSalvo. This is a most unexpected surprise. How can I be of help?" came the concerned reply of the Native American sitting in Santa Fe, New Mexico, with her morning coffee.

"President Silver Moon, as you might expect my call is one of considerable need. Specifically, my Rome center needs the services of your Lictor of Magic."

Blinking in surprise at the request, the president of TIIIS said, "That sounds serious Mr. Chairman. Do you want to tell me why you need our Lictor of Magic?"

DeSalvo sighed heavily. "Our Rome center is under attack by a rogue vampire. It has already killed four of our membership and three of our vampire hunters. Frankly, Madam President, this threat is beyond our current security capabilities."

Silver Moon sat back in her office chair and just stared back in shock at her colleague half a world away. The man had just admitted he was defenseless. It took her several moments to digest that fact.

"Madam President, I do believe that your organization is in our debt. We sent our best telekinetic sensitives to you during the asteroid crisis, Project Damokles. I now formally petition you for the use of your enforcer."

Silver Moon recognized the debt and nodded in acknowledgment. "You're on, Mr. Chairman. I will send Stone forthwith. But first, tell me about your problem so that I can better brief him."

What the TIIIS president did not tell him was the Vatican, specifically Cardinal Alberti, had already requested help to address what the cleric had characterized as "quite a mess." As with CMES, the Vatican had asked for the same assistance. *Rogue vampire? Just what in God's name is going on in Rome?*

CHAPTER 14

Those who make up the paranormal world are a tightly-knit band, even among blood enemies. They have to be given their sparse numbers. Outsiders often fail to understand, much less appreciate, this age-old fact.

For the Hidden Folk, and sensitives in general, information was the currency of their entire system—from the news of alliances made or broken, newly-devised spells or potions, to the telling of lurid gossip and the sharing of outlandish rumor. A favor asked was almost always granted, while the debt of a favor given was never forgotten. Similarly, the strict rules of hospitality most often kept the peace and mended fences.

As Dannica began the stalk of her father, she realized she needed help. As the monster hunter slowly sauntered through the early evening hustle and bustle of Rome's cramped inner city, certain coven signs stuck out to her, being left in plain sight, as no outsider would ever notice them.

Open-air markets were ideal and the best place to leave messages, precisely because they were the neighborhood's nexus. Depending upon the fruit, vegetable, fish, bread, spice, or meat on display, fragmentary information was shared like newspaper headlines for those who knew what they were looking for. To receive "the rest of the story," a minor purchase followed by a short conversation was all that was needed. But in times of emergency or distress, the information shown was completely available and free for the asking.

This is how Dannica got wind of her father's passing. Extremely accurate descriptions of him were expressed as street gossip about the possibility of a movie star in Rome or the trade of a Croatian basketball player to the national Italian team.

One vegetable vendor, a middle-aged man with large, expressive brown eyes, outright confronted her as she passed by his wheeled stall.

"You there," he motioned, "hunter of many *things*, you need to be aware of the passing of potential quarry."

"So, observant one, how much for this fine celery of yours?"

"One Euro per bunch."

After some thought, "That seems quite fair," Dannica said handing over the coin and receiving her celery wrapped in newspaper in return. "So tell me about this 'potential quarry'."

"Tall, fit, handsome. Sound familiar?"

"Perhaps. What else?"

"He was in a hurry, nearly jogging, going in that direction," the vendor gestured with his head.

"When?"

"Two days ago."

Dannica passed the vendor another Euro.

"What is this?"

"A thank you."

"Blessings upon you, hunter of many *things*. May I make a suggestion?"

"Certainly."

"Make a visit to the bread seller over there. Tell the woman that Luis sent you. I think the news that she has will be of interest to you."

"Thank you Luis. You are a dear."

After Dannica got through purchasing a small loaf of Etruscan rustic from the bread vendor, "the news" was about several attacks upon the membership of the CMES coven and the current lockdown of its central headquarters. As to who or what was responsible for all the carnage, Dannica had no doubt.

*　　*　　*

Following his conversation with the cardinal, Reissen

sat in his office, troubled over the loss of the two Vatican colleagues. Frankly, he really did not know Brian or Adela that well, but he knew them well enough to easily pick them out of a crowd. But the subject of lethality was not something the archaeologist easily associated with Pro Deo. That was more the purview of the Brothers of St. Paul. But given what had happened to him over that past two years in Egypt, and now in Rome, Reissen had to admit sudden death was in the cards.

This grim train of thought was broken by the buzzing of his office phone.

"Dr. Reissen," a breathless Dannica said, "This is Dr. Ruthmann. I know where my father is."

"You do?"

"Yes, he is besieging the CMES headquarters in Rome."

"'Besieging?' How can one individual do that?"

"He has already killed seven of this coven's membership, and now the entire villa is in a defensive posture, that's how."

"Give me your location Dr. Ruthmann, and I will get there as soon as possible."

"Thank you, Dr. Reissen. I knew you would understand."

As the Austrian hurriedly left his office, he had to immediately stop and return to retrieve his forgotten 9mm automatic. With the stiff weight of the weapon pressing against his left ribcage, he thought, *and this is precisely why your current job can be lethal.*

*   *   *

Mid-flight, Jonathan Joseph Stone caught himself snoring. With a parched throat, he sat up from the reclined leather seat, rubbed his eyes, stretched, and made for the jet cabin's counter for a bottle of water. Having drained it, he went to the head, brushed his teeth, and washed his face. Bent over and looking into the tiny mirror, the six-three Texan said, "Well old man, you are getting a bit old for this kind of jet-setting," as he fingered his graying hair.

Returning to the main cabin of the Gulfstream V, TIIIS' private jet, Stone opened up his laptop, checked his email, and then returned to the brief that his boss, President Betsy Silver Moon, had sent him. Apparently, both the Vatican *and* CMES had requested TIIIS to deploy him to Rome to destroy a troublesome vampire. That was it—a quick in and out, seek and destroy mission.

After reading the brief for the fifth time, Stone

grunted, and began to wonder about things like: why? who? where? and since when were the Vatican *and* CMES incapable of running down such creatures? And on top of that, neither organization even knew where the perp was, just the vague possibility that it might be hanging around a certain neighborhood.

The once highly-decorated US Marine sergeant knew BS when he saw it, and consequently, was extremely leery of this entire deployment. Politics and intrigue were *surely* involved.

As for the First Soul, a primeval entity that Stone was uniquely born with, it too was flummoxed with the situation. All it could do for the moment was caution patience and cool-headedness. *Soul carrier. Do your job. Let others spin their entangling webs.*

So, orders were orders. J.J. Stone, the protector of good and enforcer of divine order, was resigned to fulfill this assignment. His job as the TIIIS Lictor of Magic was to destroy that which was evil, be they demons, witches, or as in this case, a vampire. Protected by his UCS—Urban Combat Suit, and armed with a silver-ceramic sword dedicated to his auric touch, and other tactical goodies, he was ready for anything.

* * *

The daylight had become dusky dark by the time the archaeologist arrived.

"Thank you for coming Dr. Reissen." Dannica earnestly said, standing from within the shadow of a private residence's portico.

"So where is the CMES headquarters?"

The monster hunter pointed, "About two hundred meters in that direction. It is an isolated villa atop a barren hill."

"Okay. Have you seen your father?"

"No."

"Can you smell him?"

"No."

"So why are we here?"

"Because seven individuals have died at his hands. I have no solid proof of that fact, just street gossip that seven were found dead in front of the villa, all taken by a vampire."

"All at once?"

"No. Piecemeal. One at a time."

"I see. That is rather thin Dr. Ruthmann."

"I know."

Alright, might I suggest that we, together, take a walk?"

"Where?"

"Just follow me," the archaeologist said, dressed in casual summer wear with a thin windbreaker. He stuck both hands into his windbreaker's pockets and started toward the villa's neighborhood. "Take my arm," he ordered. She did and together they slowly strolled. For all appearances, they made an attractive couple.

"I am depending on you to scent your father," Reissen said conversationally. "And, since when does a monster hunter shy away from a stalk?"

Dannica did not say a word.

"Dr. Ruthmann, I want an answer."

"For the first time, in a long time, I am unsure of myself."

"Why?"

"My father is very ancient Dr. Reissen. I have never encountered anyone quite like him."

At that, Reissen stopped and turned to face his companion.

"So, here we are. For some reason you called me to join you here. Lured me into a potentially dangerous situation, and now you say you are scared."

Reissen stared hard into her eyes. "Just who and what are you?"

"I am Dr. Dannica Ruthmann … an ancient dhampirica. You know this."

"First off, your title is a fiction. I checked. There is no Ruthmann on the Milano faculty."

Dannica just shrugged.

Reissen's face wrinkled into a sneer. "For that matter, at this moment you do not impress me as a dhampirica either. Ruthmann, Dannica, Astra, whatever your name is, your entire attitude is all wrong. I know, because I hunted with my father since I was a boy."

Then Dannica's nostrils flared and eyes glazed over. "Beware. He is near." The monster hunter went for her knife.

* * *

Stone's transfer from the Leonardo da Vinci Airport went seamlessly. Riding in a large unmarked panel van, the Texan, who sat in the back, zipped opened his large equipment bag, stripped to the skin, and slipped into his one piece, Kevlar-based UCS. His minders were stunned as the man slowly disappeared before their very eyes as Stone's suit blended into its immediate surroundings. Once his hood and facemask were in place, sword scabbard adjusted over his left shoulder, and 9mm placed in its holster, he was ready to deploy and signaled so with a thumbs up.

"*Signore* Stone," the man wearing a black cassock

and white collar addressed him. "Your target reportedly is very tall, 212 centimeters, with long black hair, and broad shoulders. Destroy him with extreme prejudice," the priest coldly told him.

Through his heavily-filtered facemask, Stone asked with a muted voice, "What precisely is 212 centimeters tall in Standard?"

"Nearly seven feet tall."

Suddenly the Texan realized that his six three frame was flat out puny.

"Well Father," he rationalized, "the bigger they are, the harder they fall."

Serious silence.

"*Signore*, as soon as you complete the kill, be sure to radio us on channel 282.8, so we may evacuate you from the area." Then the priest asked the invisible man who occupied the van's rear area. "*Signore*, one last thing before we drop you off, would you like to receive the Last Rites?"

"No thank you, father, I'm a Southern Baptist. But that seven foot dude I'm after might appreciate your offer more."

Again with that "serious" silence.

Moments later the van slowed to a stop, and its huge right side cargo door slid open. No sooner than

Stone cleared the van, it sped off leaving the TIIIS Lictor of Magic standing in the middle of a deserted cobblestoned lane. It was early evening. The stars were still struggling to come out.

Stone settled down into a low defensive crouch and slowly spun around on the balls of his feet. The TIIIS agent tapped the side of his facemask, adjusting his goggles to the green world of night vision. All around him was a posh neighborhood filled with flower gardens, clumps of mature pine, luxuriant and well-trimmed shrubberies, and impressive structures. But one property, a low rambling villa directly opposite him, stood out starkly as it was perched on a barren mound devoid of any vegetation. The red dots of its many overlapping security cameras were self-evident.

"Jesus H. Christ!" he mumbled to himself. "I know that villa! It's the CMES headquarters!"

Focus, soul carrier, the First Soul interrupted. *The monster that we seek is about. Can you not sense its presence?* The Texan perceived the observation much like an intimate whisper.

Automatically, Stone reached up with his left hand and slowly drew his Bone Sword from its scabbard on his back. Simultaneously, he reached out with all six of his senses and was rewarded with the sensation of a

gentle disturbance to his right. At that very moment, a
dog howled mournfully in the distance.

CHAPTER 15

Reissen and Dannica stood back-to-back in the middle of the cobblestone lane. The only illumination came from the neighbors' entranceway lamps and windows, but none of it extended onto the darkened lane.

"Where?" Reissen dared to murmur.

"Somewhere in front of me."

*   *   *

Quiet as a ghost, Stone padded down the same cobblestone lane on his soft, rubber-soled boots. Unfortunately, his facemask's filtration prevented him from enjoying the heady scents of the flowerbeds that he passed by. With his head on a swivel, his night vision picked up two individuals—a man and a woman, standing stiffly in the lane's center in a back-to-back, clearly defensive posture. Neither of these two was anywhere near seven feet tall. Instead, both were closer to six-two—tall enough for Italians. Or were they? There was something about the guy on the right that rang a bell.

Stone continued scanning the area. Then he saw it, all seven foot of it, standing in front of the woman on the left in a dark shadow. He estimated the big guy was about twenty yards from her. *The priest wasn't kidding. This guy is not only big, but looks ripped as hell.*

At this point, the Lictor of Magic blocked his mind from any telepath intrusions or leakage. His breathing slowed. His grip on the Bone Sword firmed. Stone's forward motion eased across the pavement like a rattle snake in high grass. It was extremely important that no one detected him. That meant that no one could give him away. The words of his briefing, "in and out as quickly as you can," echoed in his consciousness. Only then did he translocate—a neat trick some very special rodents had taught him—to pass near the target and between it and the woman.

*   *   *

Sigmund was so thoroughly surprised he had halted his hunt to consider the situation. There, in the middle of the road, stood that vixen of a daughter. Now full grown, her beauty had stopped him cold. The sensitive with her would make a good meal, but as for her …

The ancient vampire sensed the sudden shift in air pressure, a virtual bow wave, and instantly reacted like Gumby by leaning back in a deep, back-breaking arch. It was good he had.

*   *   *

The tip of Stone's Bone Sword only made a half-inch nick in the bridge of the vampire's nose as he passed by, instead of cleaving Sigmund's neck from his body. Nonetheless, the sheer impact of the blow created a cloud of red mist that hung in the air and dotted the vampire's face. The stunned target grunted and violently shook his head to clear it.

*   *   *

Dannica saw her father standing there in the deep shadows. Reflexively she drew her silver knife from within her light leather jacket and prepared for the worst. Then Sigmund jerked himself backward into an impossible backbend just as something, or someone, had struck him on the nose, causing him to snort, hiss loudly in pain, and shake his head.

*   *   *

Missed, dammit!

This time, don't go slow ... go low ...

Stone began his swing and again translocated, this time in a low stance, his sword cocked over his right shoulder. The impact jarred the Lictor of Magic to his core, but he maintained his stroke and follow through as if practicing against a particularly stout swordsman's pell.

*　*　*

To their horror, Dannica and Reissen witnessed the separation of the vampire at the trunk. Blood and guts flew in a vapor-like trail that led to a barely visible figure, which stood some ten yards away. Gore covered him from head to toe. Then, without a word, the unknown slid something over his left shoulder, removed an object from his hip, and strode silently over to the fallen vampire. Wordlessly, he pumped three muffled rounds into its screaming head. Now a ruined mess, and with silence again restored, a large white panel van appeared with its side door wide open.

Before the stranger disappeared into it, he turned to address the couple in a Texan accent, "Good to see you again Dr. Reissen, but I wouldn't stick around if I was you. A cleanup crew is on their way and I don't know what their tactical protocol is for witnesses."

*　*　*

"Just who was *that*?" Dannica pointed at the departing van, nearly screaming in Reissen's ear.

The archaeologist frowned, "I really cannot say."

"But he obviously knows you!"

"Yes. That appears to be so …"

Just then, twelve men dressed like an urban SWAT team appeared. Three carried portable wet-vacs, two came with filled soapy buckets, and two toted large floor brooms. Two—probably medics from the surgical gloves that they wore, struggled with filling the body bag between them with the rapidly deteriorating body parts of the fallen vampire. The final three, heavily-armed, formed a triangle around the scene facing outward. They worked quickly, silently, and efficiently in a manner that suggested this was not their first rodeo. Within minutes they were finished. Only wet cobblestones brushed clean remained, smelling distinctly of bleach. As for the twelve, they jogged over to the villa on the barren hill and disappeared single-file through an open doorway.

Dannica and Reissen just stared in disbelief during the entire process.

"Did I just see that happen?" the monster hunter murmured.

"A quick kill followed by sanitization of the kill zone. I would say someone wants this kept very quiet," the archaeologist said, perhaps a bit too clinically.

Turning to Dannica the Austrian then said, "I think that this would be a good time to leave."

"I agree."

They left the quite neighborhood the same way they arrived—arm-in-arm.

"Care for a stiff drink?" Reissen asked. "I may need several after that display of blood and guts."

"Only if it is Grappa."

CHAPTER 15

The following morning Reissen received a call from Cardinal Alberti's office requesting his presence. Curious, Reissen replied that he would be right over.

The archaeologist, a consummate empath, did not need a bright yellow road sign with an exclamation point when he entered the cardinal's office suite. Father Joseph, uncharacteristically, did not meet his gaze and spoke little. Upon placing his hand on the wooden panel of the cleric's office door, it felt on fire.

Standing before the cardinal's desk with his hands behind him, Reissen was made to wait while his superior finished brutally typing a message on his laptop.

Finally, now with his hands folded before him, his face quite flushed, Cardinal Alberti looked his charge straight in the eye. "Dr. Reissen. Are you a covert member of The Brothers of St. Paul?"

"No, Your Eminence," the archaeologist answered.

"Indeed you are not! For the good Brothers of St. Paul represent the tactical side for *all* paranormal Vatican business. Allow me to remind *you* that as a member of Pro Deo, you are primarily a research resource. Is that clear, Dr. Reissen?"

"Crystal, Your Eminence."

"Good. Now, kindly tell me what you were doing last night in the company of a dhampirica in the neighborhood of the CMES headquarters?"

"Frankly, Your Eminence, upon reflection, I cannot say."

"Well then, Dr. Reissen, allow me to fill you in." The cleric raised his right hand with splayed fingers. "First, were you armed?"

"Yes, Your Eminence."

"So you intentionally acted suspecting the need for a weapon?"

"Yes, Your Eminence."

"Second," now gripping another finger, "you knowingly put yourself into jeopardy by accompanying a dhampirica on the hunt. Is that not so?"

"Yes, Your Eminence."

"Third, because of your presence at the scene of the vampire's destruction, you witnessed far too much. Your life was spared, however, and now I, Cardinal Alberti, owe that Godless coven's chairman, CMES, not one, but two life-debts."

The cleric paused as his refolded hands now had already lost much of their blood.

"Fourth, Dr. Reissen, in order to preserve some

semblance of dignity for our department, I asked an outside entity to destroy the vampire, instead of requesting The Brothers of St. Paul to perform the act."

"Are you referring to the TIIIS Lictor of Magic, Your Eminence?"

The cardinal nodded stiffly, face beet-red. "How did you know?"

"Stone is the only invisible man that I know of with such a dreadful Texan accent."

A grunt and a nod. "Indeed."

After another moment, "Dr. Reissen. What you did last night reflected poorly upon this department. Am I clear?"

"Yes, Your Eminence."

The cleric sighed deeply. "That is all, Dr. Reissen. And no more unauthorized adventures."

"Yes, Your Eminence."

As the Austrian walked back to his office feeling several centimeters shorter, he began to realize that the internal politics of the Vatican could not compare in any way to those of his old university. Cardinal Alberti had gambled on the Albanian vampire remains not only by investigating them, but also by bringing them back to the museum. Two forensic technicians had died because of that decision. Lord only knows how many more innocents died at the vampire's hands. Dannica had *only* mentioned seven. Her providential appearance represented a possible answer for the vampire's destruction to the cardinal, but one that appeared far too late in the game. Apparently, he had already made his decision beforehand, and went with a proven solution—Stone.

*   *   *

"What are the odds of reviving this monster?" William DeSalvo, the international chairman of CMES, wanted to know.

Dr. Giuseppe Marvo had never before been asked such a question, much less undertaken the premise. His seminal work was primarily with the extension of life, not its revival. With advanced degrees in biology and chemistry, his chairman was asking him to be, in essence, Dr. Frankenstein.

"No promises, *Signor Presidente*. The damage to the skull was quite extensive. But once we piece it together, if we immerse the corpse in the proper nutrients, who knows?" he concluded with upraised and open hands.

As the physician stood there with his hands on hips, he finally worked up the courage to ask, "*Signor*

Presidente. I well know that it is not my place, but why resurrect such a monster? It has already claimed seven of our members."

"You are correct, Dr. Marvo. That question is indeed beyond your place. Now, do your best with this project."

"*Sì, Signor Presidente.* I will try my best."

*   *   *

Stone's debrief took place on TIIIS' Old Oak campus in southwestern Pennsylvania. It was their organization's wooded bastion of academic training for sensitives of all stripes. Within Old Main, in a stuffy office, the Lictor of Magic met with his president, Betsy Silver Moon.

"Okay, I'm back from Rome all safe and sound."

"And I am glad for it," Silver Moon remarked. "I was none too happy about that assignment."

"How so?" the Texan asked.

"I just went down so quickly, and with not one, but two requests for us to intervene. Frankly, I fully expected some sort of a setup. Did you see anything out-of-the-ordinary?"

"Other than cutting down a giant of a vampire, not

really. But I did notice a remarkable amount of efficient haste, or maybe just eagerness on the part of the Vatican, to get me in and out quickly."

"Interesting."

"And then there was this comment made by the priest in the van, just before they deployed me at the kill site, that a cleanup crew would show up as soon as I was finished."

"A cleanup crew … now that does not sound like the Vatican," Silver Moon remarked. "Not that they are not very good at covering up their tracks. In fact, they can be quite elegant. But a cleanup crew, that's just too utilitarian for them. J.J., did you ever see any Vatican documentation?"

"Nope. Never. Just a priest who wanted to give me my Last Rites."

"Is it possible, J.J., that the Vatican did not pick you up at the airport?"

Now blinking at the idea, Stone said, "Completely possible. I just assumed that they were Vatican because of one guy with a white collar."

"Did that man perhaps posing as a priest say anything out-of-character to you, J.J.?"

"Yeah, he was all business Betsy. Like no priest I ever met. All hatchet-faced and totally into the take down. What did he say to me … yeah, now I remember, 'destroy him with extreme prejudice.' A pretty cold-blooded statement for a priest to make."

"The reason I am pursuing this train of thought J.J., is because Cardinal Alberti, who initially contacted me, just informed me that his people never picked you up at the airport."

"What?" Stone exclaimed. "Then who did?"

"Precisely my point J.J."

*   *   *

"Cardinal Alberti," Father Joseph fretted while rubbing his hands together, "I forgot to inform you that yesterday *Signore* Stone was not at the airport when I arrived to pick him up. The gate agent said that someone else from the Vatican had done so."

The cardinal, uncharacteristically, just stared back at his assistant. In his mind, an unraveling of details and events was rapidly occurring. The cleric rubbed at his temples in an unconscious attempt to drain off what he suspected.

"Your Eminence?" Father Joseph prompted.

In response, the cardinal just waved his hand as if shooing away a fly. "I find, my son, that there is just so very much on my mind." Smiling, "but thank you for that bit of information. It truly explains much."

Now once again alone in his office, the cleric looked around and took it all in. For some reason he wondered whether a member of the laity would ever sit in his office. Reissen, naturally, came to mind. Such a bright and decisive man, so full of creativity and life.

CHAPTER 16

Sigmund indeed revived. Once his skull and skeleton were repaired, it was just a matter of bathing it in a bloody cocktail of nutrients. Four days later he was judged fully-functional—actually, quite robust, for never in the wild had the vampire enjoyed such nourishment and in such quantities. His body mass had filled out, his black curly hair grown long, and his skin glowed with a deep golden hue. Physically Sigmund was once again in his prime.

The real question remained about the state of his mind. It needed to be asked. The first order of business was communication. Only once had the security tapes captured anything said by the vampire and that was a crude form of Latin. Other than that there were no other clues. Further, extreme care was used by all who came in contact with him. No one knew whether he was telepathic. The only thing that was known, abundantly, was his abiding hatred for CMES. As a consequence, nothing was said or thought about where he was or who had revived him.

The location for the revival process was a private clinic located outside of Geneva, Switzerland. The "patient" resided in a four room private suite typically used by those who wished to change their physical attributes. Such "patients", like Sigmund, were afforded extreme discretion and privacy. Within this particular facility such things were a commonplace, and internal and external security was top notch.

Lightly sedated and restrained to a bed, a procession of linguists came and went, hoping to be the one to first break through. Modern European languages caused not one flicker of recognition in the monster's dilated eyes. Entreaties in Arabic, in several dialects, were similarly ignored. Several Far Eastern experts elicited no response. But when a Classicist entered the room, sat down, and requested his name in Latin, it was as if a light bulb had been turned on. The spoken Latin seemed to enliven the vampire, who identified himself as Sigmund—a name of unquestionable Germanic origin.

Next, a strong red wine was provided and the vampire's conversation became fluid and mellifluous. The interrogator avoided embarrassing topics, instead getting the now very drunk and sedated vampire to reminisce about sundry subjects of the times. An ancient historian and specialist of the Early Roman Empire, the man just listened to this being rant and rave about the religions and politics of the period. For this staid university professor, listening was pure joy. His extensive note-taking became far more than a dry info dump. Instead, the scholar was asking questions that bedeviled his field. Things like "What did the sunshades of the Coliseum look like?" "Did sea battles actually take place within its arena?" "Had he ever heard of an author named Suetonius?" The monster's answer surprised the professor. "Suetonius? What a muckraker of gossip and rumor. He would do and write anything to be invited to a sumptuous dinner party."

During another choice rant, Sigmund revealed much. "Caracalla, what a prig!" he railed. "That worthless pile of donkey excrement hated us all! He even went after our coven! Said that *we* were a subversive faction set against the empire. The bastard even sent the Praetorian Guard to round us up. Did we fix that! Had those mealy-mouthed Christians take it in the arse instead of us! Served them right! All that nonsense about eternal life! Touting the blood of the Christ! What did they know? And all the while not one of their kind was a vampire!"

* * *

"*Signor Presidente*, we now know who the vampire is. His name is Sigmund, a rogue vampire from our second century. The reason he attacked the Rome center was because he was once a coven member who our council subsequently ordered to be tortured and buried alive. We even have the council's proceedings concerning the creature in the archives. Frankly, sir, he single-handedly caused more than he is worth."

"That's very interesting, *Signore* Gnotti. What did he do to so royally piss off the council?"

"Basically, *Signor Presidente*, indiscriminate predation of the Rome mob. Apparently he was quite sloppy, was told to desist, and he told them to bugger off. In response, forty judges were dispatched to take care of the matter."

"Forty?"

"Yes, and only eight of them returned. Even in those days the monster was quite formidable," Gnotti mentioned.

"Perfect, just perfect. Now how is his re-education progressing?"

"Short-term memory is extremely sketchy, long-term memory is intact, and I am told, quite colorful. He seems to be a perfect candidate for reintegration."

"Then get to it, *Signore* Gnotti. I have plans for him."

I just thought you might, Gnotti smiled back.

CHAPTER 17

Klaus Mendenhall Rubin, the Swiss classicist who had
successfully made contact with Sigmund, became the
vampire's conversation partner. As a result, he had the
task of teaching the vampire spoken English, since
CMES judged that to be the most useful modern
language for him to learn. Up to the task, Rubin devised
flashcards that subtly mixed the familiar with the new.

Pater = father
Mater = mother
Frater = brother
Habeo = to have
Esse = to be
Fortuna = luck
Annum = year
Ira = anger
Patria = homeland
Pecunia = money
Amica = friend
Inimicus = enemy
Vita = life
Puella = girl
Quam = how
Quid = what
Quod = when
Puer = boy
Femina = woman
Vir = man
Exitus = exit
Porta = entrance

Rubin then began cleverly playing with the words, constructing rudimentary English sentences and rude jokes based upon the English verb "to be" and its irregular Latin equivalent "*esse*."

I am = *sum*
You are = *es*
He/she/it = *est*
We are = *sumus*
You are = *estis*
They are = *sunt*

To the classicist's pleasure, Sigmund rapidly caught on to what the philologist was trying to impart. Over the next several days, the vampire's vocabulary grew as he pointed to all the objects in his suite. His facility to understand and translate his thoughts into English did as well.

The most difficult concept to get across to Sigmund was the passage of time. This led Rubin into a discussion of numbers, calculations, and finally chronology. When the light bulb finally brightened in Sigmund's eyes, the vampire bowed his head in thought.

"Friend Rubin. How many years am I?"

"More than eighteen hundred years."

That answer raised the vampire's heavy eyebrows.

"What have I missed, friend Rubin?"

The scholar stopped himself to calculate. "More than ninety lifetimes."

The vampire groaned at the number and looked despondent.

"What troubles you so, Sigmund? You are immortal. You have more than enough time to catch up."

*   *   *

By week's end, Sigmund finally asked Rubin the sixty-four dollar question. "Friend Rubin, why am I here?"

"A good question, Sigmund. Do you wish revenge against those who injured you?"

"Yes. They did great injury to me," the vampire stated with absolute fire in his eyes. "How do I find my enemies?"

Rubin rubbed his chin in thought, not so much about the answer that his superiors wanted him to plant within the vampire's psyche, but its legitimacy. The classicist was torn. He befriended this monster and earned its trust and maybe respect. While Rubin suspected he was not telepathic, Sigmund was definitely a bright empath who could easily detect a lie, if not outright smell it from his pores.

"Sigmund, you have many enemies. Some fear

you. Others hate you. The enemies that injured you are in Rome."

The monster internally translated the word to *Roma* and let out a low growl. "Who are they?"

"They are many. They live within Rome in a walled quarter called the Vatican. They, Sigmund, were the ones who injured you."

"When can I seek my revenge?"

"When you can speak English very well."

"How long will that take?"

"That is your decision. Work hard and you will be able to go sooner."

"I work hard, friend Rubin."

"Good. And I will help you."

"Good! Friend Rubin."

*   *   *

Four intense weeks later, Sigmund was deemed passable within modern society. The vampire's grasp of language was astounding. It had an inquisitive mind, asked questions that sometimes stumped Rubin, and generally marveled with modern-day commonplaces with child-like joy. Automobiles fascinated him with all of their workings. On his first ride with the classicist, Sigmund stuck his head and shoulders out the open window like a puppy. Airplanes that passed high overhead caused another jaw-dropping reaction and observation. "Their wings do not move, friend Rubin. How is that?"

*   *   *

"He is ready to deploy, *Signore* Gnotti," the classicist said over the encrypted phone.

"Are you sure Dr. Rubin?"

"As best as I can be. The only things that will attract people's attention to him are his extreme stature and striking good looks. To cover this, Sigmund enjoys pretending to be a movie star. This appeals to his ego."

"He knows what a movie star is?"

"Of course, *signore*. His favorite film is *Gladiator*. He adores Russell Crowe's role in it and identifies directly with the six-six Germanic warrior, Hagen, played by Ralf Moeller. Of course, he pointed out to me several errors with the movie, specifically with the Coliseum itself."

"You discuss such things in English?"

"*Sì, Signore* Gnotti, of course. Naturally he has his lapses, times when his vocabulary fails him, but overall, Sigmund is quite fluent. I would judge his reading ability as that of an eleven-year-old native speaker."

"If you had to guess what nationality he is, what would his passport say?"

"Definitely German. His heavy, thick Latin accent fits that national designation quite well."

"Interesting, very interesting … and well done Dr. Rubin."

"Thank you, *signore*."

*   *   *

Three days later, CMES provided Rubin with Sigmund's passport, credit card, and several other necessary documents. Rubin explained to Sigmund the function of each and their value.

As Sigmund fingered the pretty color holographic image on his credit card, he said, "Such a small thing that does so much."

"Indeed," Rubin nodded. "It represents the buying power of one hundred thousand *aurei*."

"Truly!" said the vampire using his latest favorite expression. "With such money, I could by a villa."

"Not quite, but a good portion of it," Rubin corrected.

Then the vampire asked a question that the classicist had not expected.

"Why did you do this for me?"

"To exact vengeance against the Vatican."

"No," the vampire shook his head. "Vengeance is only mine to savor. Why have *you* helped me?"

"Because," Rubin replied with a serious look, "your enemies are mine as well."

"Ah, now I understand. I am your soldier, something to train and put to war."

"Not entirely. When you have had your fill of blood and vengeance, I look forward to a time when we, together, can discuss many things."

"Truly, I would like that, friend Rubin."

*   *   *

Rubin had one last task—to accompany Sigmund from Geneva to Rome. Thereafter, the vampire was on his own. For the odd pair, as Rubin was a short, portly, red-haired man, the classicist made it a grand game as if the two of them were in a movie.

The first step was the purchase of comfort class tickets for the nearly eight-hour train journey. These they bought separately and at different counters to test out the vampire's passport, credit card, and signature, which he had laboriously struggled to learn to do. They departed in the early afternoon. Their arrival would be around nine that evening.

Step two was Sigmund's socialization. Drinking blood from a plastic bladder had become a boring necessity if the vampire had any hope of controlling himself within any confined spaces that contained mortals, that is, prey. The challenge, that Rubin intellectually understood but could not appreciate, was the vampire's senses had to be tamed as they were so attuned to the hunt. A racing heartbeat, the smell of fear, nervous sweat, and the sheer empathic reading of the weak, were all things that Sigmund had to control.

To distract Sigmund's senses, Rubin provided him with a compact recorder and top-of-the-line Bois headphones, specially chosen for his charge's acute hearing. Among the recordings that the Swiss included were soothing tracks—Copland's *Appalachian Spring*, several haunting Lakota flute works by J.J. Kent, *Clair de Lune* by Debussy, a sampling of smooth jazz, a handful of ballads by Enya, an entire disk devoted to classical music at the movies, and finally, Rachmaninoff's *Rhapsody on a Theme of Paganini*, piano concerto number one.

The vampire was absolutely smitten by Rubin's gift, and often was observed gently swaying to the music with a blissful smile. The train ride from Geneva to Rome went quickly and uneventfully.

Standing on the Rome train platform, Rubin genuinely hugged the hulking vampire. With tears in his eyes, "My good friend. I wish you only the best of hunting! Be strong, brave, and as unstoppable as Hagen."

Sigmund cocked his head to one side. "What do you mean by 'unstoppable'?"

"How many arrows did it take to kill Hagen?"

After a moment of thought, "Six."

"Be like Hagen!"

"Thank you, friend Rubin." The vampire grinned. "I shall."

CHAPTER 18

As Rubin watched Sigmund casually disappear into the *Roma Termini* train station—as if that were even possible—the classicist smiled as his former student had to duck down under the arch of the passageway. He then pulled out his device and made a call.

"*Ciao* Gnotti."

"It is done." So began CMES' revenge upon the Roman Church for their falsely perceived role in the coven's decline.

*   *   *

The newly liberated vampire eagerly confronted his first challenge—how to navigate the train station's vast labyrinth. Fortunately, a schematic map appeared on one wall. Seeing a red circle in the center of the map that he understood as, "You are here," Sigmund plotted his route out to Vatican City. By his reckoning, a train ride via the red-coded Metro A, toward Battistini, and with a stop at *Cipro Musei Vaticani*, would take him about twenty minutes. Now all he needed to do was purchase a ticket, a process that he had already accomplished in Geneva. While searching for a ticket kiosk, he paused at a hat vendor. While he did not find a sunhat he liked, he *did* purchase a black broad-brimmed hat with his credit card that said "Stetson, Size 23" on its interior band. It fit him perfectly.

*   *   *

Forty minutes later an extremely tall man, made even taller by a cowboy hat, stood before the *Musei Vaticani*, and to his surprise, he found he that could easily read the many Latin architectural inscriptions. While the museum was closed at that hour of the night—close to ten o'clock, the nearby neighborhood remained lively with café's, restaurants, and bistros. Couples strolled hand-in-hand, sometimes arm-in-arm. Flower vendors did a lively trade.

Strangely, the vampire took a pass and ignored them all. Yet in another time he would have thought nothing of openly culling several. The reason that he did not was because he had been purposefully spoiled during his most recent resurrection. His taste for blood had been altered. No longer was he a survivalist bottom feeder where anything would do. Instead, he had been raised on countless pints of blood donated by CMES's most powerful adepts and sensitives. Put another way that mortals might better understand—a bottle of Charles Shaw, "Two Buck Chuck," no longer was good enough for his palate. But a heady, dense, and fragrant Malbec from Argentina's Mendoza region would do just fine.

So that evening Sigmund checked into the hotel that his friend Rubin had thoughtfully reserved for him, complete with a king-sized bed. Opening its windows, the vampire allowed the scents of Rome to envelope him. They were all so delicious. Friend Rubin had told him that many long-lived and evil adepts and sensitives worked within the Vatican. It was they who had injured him so. He smiled into the night, for tomorrow he would make a visit they would never forget.

* * *

Rubin had also prepaid Sigmund's tickets to the Vatican's many museums. The vampire's role was that of a tourist on holiday, so he dressed the part in black sneakers, jeans, a black collarless shirt, matching cloth jacket, and of course his most recent acquisition—the black broad-brimmed hat.

As he walked toward the Vatican's entrance in the morning sun, Sigmund turned up his jacket's collar to protect his neck and the sides of his face, while he jammed his exposed hands into his jacket's side pockets.

Once safely within the shade of the *Musei Vaticani*'s walls, the vampire readjusted his collar, yielded his ticket to the security guard, and entered the hallowed halls filled with art. In an attempt to blend in, Sigmund followed a tour led by a museum docent, half-listening, half-scenting for potential high-profile victims.

Forty minutes into the tour, the vampire found himself listening more and more, and in the process, appreciating the passage of time. Sigmund also suspected that his friend Rubin had wanted him to discover this on his own. Sigmund alternately felt pangs of familiarity to outright laughter at some of the outlandish comments made by the docent, not surprisingly, given the nature of the artifacts displayed—Roman, Byzantine, Renaissance, and Enlightenment.

The tour visited the Gregorian Museum next, filled with ancient Near Eastern, Egyptian, and Greek artifacts. While grandly displayed, Sigmund lost interest quickly as his nose had detected prey within. Leaving the tour while the leader was distracted, the vampire began his stalk along an administrative hallway that led away from the collections.

With his senses on full alert he came upon an open

doorway with a small bronze name plate that said:

Gabriella, Sr. Mary, OP.

One final whiff of confirmation and the vampire finally faced one of his tormentors at last. Standing at the office's threshold, Sigmund saw a tiny woman writing intently at her desk. She was dressed oddly in black robes which he understood, but also a stiffly starched bib and headpiece with a veiled head covering.

After some moments she looked up, and up, and up to take in the tall visitor at her doorway. Very slowly the nun put down her black fountain pen and folded her hands.

"My, my," Sister Gabriella said in English, "what have we here? An American cowboy? Have you lost your tour, son?"

When Sigmund saw the nun's icy blue eye and the white mass of cataract of its twin, he unconsciously stepped back and hissed.

To this reaction, Sister Gabriella stood behind her desk and began to mumble a string of Latin words—a rudimentary protective spell.

Sigmund understood and realized that he had come across not a mere sensitive for his first vengeful act, or a highly-trained adept, but rather a full-blown witch.

Lacking any implements of silver within easy reach, Sister Gabriella swore at her lack of preparation and foresight. Caught flat-footed, the feisty nun put up quite a fight nonetheless before succumbing to the vampire's saliva. During the monster's sudden rushing attack, Gabriella mustered up several underpowered psychic bolts, which charred the vampire's chest before he laid hands upon her. Once the he had fully drained his victim, Sigmund could feel the wounds closing, healing, as the nun's blood had been so powerful. From start to finish the entire three minute encounter had not been heard by anyone.

Taking in a deep breath and feeling the stretch of new flesh across his chest, Sigmund pawed at his ruined black shirt and frowned, retrieved his fallen hat, and strode out of Gabriella's office filled with a sense of victory. He murmured, "I am Hagen," as he searched for more prey.

Next, upon meeting an armed security guard in the hallway, the vampire sniffed in derision at the quality of fare and snapped his neck. Now with a fallen body on the ruddy red tile flooring, Sigmund unnecessarily kicked it viciously several times. "I am Hagen," he murmured again as he continued down the hallway in search of an object for his vengeance.

The next open door that he encountered was that of Cardinal Alberti's suite. Behind a desk sat a young priest, who upon seeing the vampire, looked up with eyes full of hope. "May I help you sir?" He asked in English after seeing the cowboy hat. "Have you lost your tour …?" Father Joseph's voice trailed off as he saw the blood weeping blast marks on the burned shirt and jacket.

Sigmund sensed some value in this young one's blood. While nowhere near the quality of the old woman's, he would do.

*   *   *

Cardinal Alberti, who sat at his desk filling out paperwork, suddenly was psychically stabbed by an intense mixture of horror, pain, and anguish from his receptionist. Then, it was gone, nothing, snuffed out. The complete lack of sensation was like a vacuum. Wide-eyed, his fingers hovering over the document in indecision, the cleric finally turned to his laptop and sent Father Joseph a message. There was no response, but now he did feel that a frightening presence stood just outside his door.

With his foot resting upon the security panic button in the floor, the cleric's wooden door frame exploded inward in an avalanche of wooden beams, boards, and flying splinters. Reflexively stabbing the panic button, Alberti knew that he was on his own until help arrived. But what crashed into his private office defied all reason and logic, a horror beyond imagination. Sigmund, his jaws dripping from the receptionist's bloodletting, charged the cardinal and took him.

Cardinal Alberti's last thoughts were a mixture of the resigned, banal, and ironic. *It was I who ordered the retrieval of his bones. It was I who saw him run off in the video. And now it is I who feeds him. Dear Lord, what have I done?*

*   *   *

Sigmund fed deeply on this one. Like the old woman he was an enormously powerful adept. So engrossed in his meal, the vampire failed to initially sense the security klaxon that blared in the hallway. Only half-finished with this one, Sigmund angrily looked up and realized that he had to flee. *What a waste!*

Then the vampire remembered what his friend Rubin had told him about his part. "Sigmund, if you ever feel that you are cornered, strip off your clothing, and run for a hiding place."

"Why strip off my clothes, Friend Rubin?"

"Because you cannot be seen on their security cameras."

Without another thought the vampire did so, leaving them throughout the cardinal's suite—even his now favorite hat.

*   *   *

Reissen heard the security klaxon and at first wondered if it was just a drill of some kind. But when a banner appeared on his laptop to exit the museum immediately, he did so with his computer under his arm. A growing crowd of tourists and staff gathered in the piazza in front of the Gregorian Museum, all the while heavily-armed security ran this way and that to their preplanned positions.

To the Austrian's surprise, neither his superior Cardinal Alberti nor his assistant Father Joseph were present among the ever-enlarging mob. It was clear to Reissen that no one knew what was going on, or for that matter, what might have happened. Panic and speculation ran rampant throughout the piazza as more and more people were added to it. This general condition then escalated sharply when a cadre of armed security formed a ring around everyone, who now stood bunched tightly together in the mid-afternoon sun.

After thirty minutes of waiting, the security force began to usher groups of twenty away from the piazza. Once outside the circle, tourists were quickly culled and led under guard outside the Vatican proper, while the staffers were directed to immediately gather in the main atrium for a security briefing

*　　*　　*

"Dear colleagues, I am Captain Lucius Abrams. We have a serious security breach," stated the ramrod straight, no nonsense, head of security. His crisp and laconic words caused all to look around.

"We have yet to find the perpetrator or perpetrators. We have nothing on the security videos."

At this admission, Reissen immediately frowned and thought, *what if?*

"So far we have four dead. Is Dr. Reissen present?"

"Yes, here I am," the archaeologist said with his arm raised.

"Good. Dr. Reissen, you will come with me. As for the rest of you, return to your offices, close down what you were doing, and go home immediately. Absolutely no exceptions. That is all."

As he was led away to the security bunker, the Austrian mentally went into the full military mode that he had learned as a young man in his homeland.

"Dr. Reissen, I have been told that you have military experience. Is that correct?"

"Yes sir."

"Are you current on your weapon?"

"Yes sir. I completed my range trials two months ago."

Now sitting down in his command cubical, Captain Lucius Abrams sighed. "Dr. Reissen, you are temporarily the operations director of Pro Deo. Cardinal Alberti had left such instructions in the event of his death. Both he and his assistant are among the dead."

Now it was Reissen's turn to sigh. "I see. What do you want me to do captain?"

"First, more bad news. One of my men had his neck broken, but Sister Mary Gabriella was also murdered—horribly."

"I need to see the bodies."

"Are you sure Dr. Reissen?"

"Absolutely."

*   *   *

All four bodies were on display in the museum's forensic laboratory. The remaining two technicians, Drs. Giffon and Lucci, fussed about trying to make the horror somehow more palatable. On entering their laboratory, Reissen and Abrams nodded to them and they stepped away from the four shrouded forms.

It took Reissen only one look at Father Joseph to realize just what they were up against. "Are the other two treated the same?" he asked Giffon and Lucci.

The two nodded.

"Are these wounds the same as you have recently seen before?"

Silent nods again.

"Were the other three cremated?"

"Yes, they were," Giffon said, "along with both Sullivan and Adams."

"Well then, we should cremate these as well … just to make sure. Have it done immediately."

"Yes, Dr. Reissen," Lucci said. "I think that would be the wisest thing to do."

Now turning to Abrams, "Have your men found anyone or thing on the grounds?"

"No sir, not yet."

Reissen pulled out his phone and started to dial.

*   *   *

"Where are you?" the Austrian tersely asked without preamble.

"In Rome, having dinner."

"How fast can you get to the Gregorian Museum?"

The archaeologist distinctly heard the subtle sound of a fork being placed on a china plate, and a call to a waiter. "Give me twenty minutes."

"Bless you."

"Is this somehow, someway, about my father?"

"Yes. See you soon."

*   *   *

"Who did you just call?" Captain Abrams asked.

"An expert."

"What kind of expert?"

"A vampire hunter."

"Are there such things?" the soldier asked incredulously.

Reissen walked over to Father Joseph's body and lifted the shroud again. "Captain. What sort of animal does this?"

"A wolf?"

"Captain, do wolves drain the blood of their victims?"

That caused the man's face to whiten.

"Are you saying …"

"Yes captain. I am. And by the way, did your men

happen to find any discarded clothing at the scene of any of the murders?"

"Yes, they did. Men's clothing."

"And have your security cameras captured any video of a tall naked man?"

"No sir."

"That is because captain, vampires do not cast shadows, they cannot create images in a mirror, and they remain invisible to photographic and digital cameras because they simply have no soul."

*   *   *

Across Rome, at a villa that rests upon a barren hillock, a man smiled as he read the online breaking news headline—"Vatican Evacuates Over Bomb Threat."

"What utter bullshit," Gnotti muttered to himself. "Sigmund is causing holy hell among the sanctimonious. The only question is, how long will his reign of terror last?"

*   *   *

Sigmund was extremely proud of himself. He had killed and fed well. He had remembered to take off his clothes just as friend Rubin had told him to do when he sensed danger. Then, the vampire hid in a place that seemed strangely familiar to him. For some reason he had gravitated to it—the basement artifact storage of the museum. Here, deep in the darkness, Sigmund found peace.

*   *   *

Reissen met Dannica at the *Musei Vaticani*'s entrance wearing a one piece tactical jumpsuit, a flack vest, and automatic pistol holstered over his left breast. In his right hand he wielded a borrowed Roman ceremonial sword—while marginally sharp, it was made of silver.

Dannica, after she exited the cab at the curb wearing jeans, a sweater, and jacket, looked the archaeologist up and down. "Not bad for an amateur. Is that made of silver?"

The Austrian snapped back, "Yes, then again, I am not the Lictor of Magic either. Please come inside. We have a desperate situation."

"Does this have anything to do with my father?"

"Actually, everything. Do you remember that cleanup crew that gathered up all your father's remains?"

"Yes, yes I do."

"Do you remember where they went?"

"Yes, the CMES villa."

"Well, my working theory is that they revived your father, and now have set him upon the Vatican."

"What proof of that do you have?"

"At the moment, none. The Vatican has cremated all the bodies that your father has touched."

"How many?"

"Four in total, with three total exsanguinations."

"That is a lot of blood. He has probably gone to ground to sleep off the gorging."

Dannica's words rang a pealing church bell in the archaeologist's mind. "You are absolutely right! And now I know where to look for him. Come on!"

*   *   *

Reissen took Dannica to the forensic laboratory first to get directions to the archaeological storage area in the museum's basement. Dr. Carlo Lucci was the only one on staff at that moment. Dr. Giffon, pulling rank, had left for the rest of the evening. The poor soul had deep dark rings around his red-rimmed eyes.

"Dr. Reissen, what are you doing back here at this late hour?"

"Well Dr. Lucci, for one I have been promoted temporarily to stand in for Cardinal Alberti. For another, we think we know where the monster is hiding in the museum."

"You do?"

"Yes, in the archeological storage area. How do we get there?"

"That's easy, I will guide you." The forensic technician then paused a beat. "I see that you are armed. What about you?" he pointedly asked Dannica, who in reply drew her silvery blade from her jacket."

Glancing between that and Reissen's sword he said, "Are you sure that is enough?"

The monster hunter's glare answered him.

"Okay, okay, but I want to bring something extra along for myself." The forensic technician took off his starched white lab coat, hung it up, and went to a locked cabinet. From it Lucci removed a short automatic weapon with a large, curved magazine.

"What is that?" Dannica pointed.

"A 45 cal. Uzi," the blushing Italian said. "I got it as a gift from an Israeli colleague of mine. Besides, with this I can chew quite a bit out of practically anything. It's the least that I can do for Brian and Adela, not to mention the others."

"Right," Reissen deadpanned. "Dr. Lucci I accept your offer of assistance. Time to go."

After five minutes the archaeologist was happy Lucci had agreed to show them the way. He had no idea how convoluted the access was to the bowels of the museum.

Lucci stopped before a pair of massive steel fire doors that were painted a dark army green. "Once we are beyond these doors, we will be in the archaeological storage area. Be advised that it is quite extensive and has no logic to its configuration. I recommend that we stay together so that no one gets lost." And with that warning, Lucci lifted the heavy latch on the door's right side and entered into pitch black darkness. Once all were inside, the forensic technician whispered, "Stop until I find the light switch."

After some tense moments, two long rows of yellowish lights illuminated and extended their radiance off into the distance.

"Wow!" the archaeologist said at the sight.

"This is only one portion of the stored collection," Lucci explained. "Are either of you Indiana Jones' fans?"

They shook their heads.

"Oh, that's too bad, because this storage area reminds me of the closing scene in the first Indy movie."

"What was that?" Dannica asked.

"And endless warehouse of shelving and wooden boxes."

"Yes, and seeing all this, I can easily envision that," the Austrian said. "Okay, everybody stick together."

And the threesome began their search for a monster.

"Dr. Ruthmann, do you smell anything?"

"Not yet Dr. Reissen. But when I do, you will be the first to know."

CHAPTER 19

Sigmund's ears perked up when they heard the opening of a metal door. Sitting up from his position on an empty length of lower shelving, the vampire concentrated trying to echo-locate where the sound had come from. Suddenly, a bank of blinding lights came on from four aisles over. Voices reached his ears—distinctly three of them. He scented the air and came up with nothing—yet. The vampire had two choices to consider. Run and escape into the night to fight another day, or, feed again. After a moment's thought he chose the latter. His hunger for vengeance had been nowhere near appeased. His stalk began.

*   *   *

The threesome moved down the aisle with the monster huntress Dannica in the lead. To their right and left were thick limestone columns that supported the museum above. Between them steel shelving stood from floor to the ceiling. Packed on these shelves, often rigged at odd levels, lay endless boxes of all kinds and sizes, each labeled. Some of the older labels were yellowed to the point of being unreadable.

The three monster hunters, with their heads on a

continuous swivel, could only see so much in their narrow canyon of archaeological artifacts. Peeking through the shelving into the adjoining aisles was a useless exercise.

"Now I know how Leonidas must have felt at Thermopylae," Reissen whispered.

About halfway down the aisle, Dannica stopped, her back stiffened and she declared, "He is near."

"How close?" Reissen asked.

"Very. In fact, he is right in front of us."

Out of the gloom, beyond where the bank lighting did not penetrate, came a nightmare. With skin the color of burnished bronze, long curly hair the color of a raven's wing, and a well-muscled physique that any weightlifter would covet, Sigmund appeared before them stark naked. Slightly bent over to pass under the low ceiling and its lighting fixtures, Sigmund growled in English, "I am Hagen. Prepare to die!" Then he charged them.

Lucci yelled back, "Just try monster," as he raised his Uzi and pulled its trigger, only to discover that the safety was in the OFF position.

Dannica brandished her silver amuletic knife, lowered herself into a fighting stance, and hissed back.

Reissen, who had distinctly heard the Uzi's trigger

click without result said, "Lucci, take your damn weapon off SAFE and put it on AUTO." Then he pulled the trigger of his 9mm. The deafening sound of the report caused the vampire to stop and cover his ears in pain, just as the round punctured his chest.

Sigmund's return howl literally vibrated their bodies. Just then, Lucci began firing short 45 cal. bursts into the vampire's center mass, staggering him back. In such close quarters, the sound of the reports were simply mind-numbing. Lucci tore literal chunks out of the vampire. Blood flooded forth and slicked the floor. Reissen, standing sideways as if in a pistol competition, continued his measured fire, striking the monster in the neck and right shoulder.

Then the creature charged. With one swing Lucci flew into a building support, bounced once, and sagged to the floor dazed. Reissen kept on firing up to the last moment, emptying his magazine, before he was slapped aside into the shelving with a loud crash.

Chest heaving, breath and blood bubbling forth from the many punctures, Sigmund took in Dannica's beauty and continued to advance. Now possessing a magnificent erection, the monster said, "Ah, my daughter! What glorious plans I have for you! You are so much like your mother."

"Never! Monster!" Dannica shrieked back, the cords of her neck straining. They grappled. They struggled for advantage. It was a standoff. So Sigmund opened his mouth to engulf Dannica's neck, but then, suddenly staggered.

Reissen took another swing with his Roman sword and hacked a second slice into the back of the monster's neck, severing its muscles. At that moment, Dannica broke her dagger hand loose and slit the vampire's throat wide open.

Now wide-eyed, Sigmund saw his daughter grab a handful of his hair and remove his head with a second stroke. His massive body hit the heavily blood-slicked floor.

Holding the separated head before her, Dannica screamed at it as his eyes fluttered and then clouded. "Now I have my revenge! For me, and for my mother! *Die* monster!"

Dropping the bloody mass on the floor, Dannica remarked, "Well done, Austrian. You will make a good monster hunter someday."

At that point, Lucci stirred back to consciousness. "What did I miss?"

*   *   *

With Lucci's assistance, the trio found a cart and took the already deteriorating remains of the vampire to the incinerator. Only when *Signore* Gappos' night assistant had finally closed the incinerator's grate and started the fire, did Reissen think about relaxing.

"Dannica, you look terrible."

"As for you, *Signore* Lucci, you need to spend more time at the range."

At that they all laughed the maniacal laugh shared only by the exhausted and insane.

CHAPTER 20

Reissen's first act as the temporary head of operations for Pro Deo was to call President Betsy Silver Moon of TIIIS. Unfortunately, he did not know her number. With the help of one of Captain Abrams men, and after several minutes on the late Cardinal Alberti's laptop, he had it at his fingertips. The archaeologist used his own phone.

Seeing the odd number on her screen, Silver Moon nonetheless greeted the stranger from her sunny Santa Fe, New Mexico office, "Hello, President Silver Moon."

After an awkward silence as he had not been prepared for such a bubbly hello, Reissen spoke. "President Silver Moon, my name is Dr. Erik Reissen. I am the interim director of operations for Pro Deo for the moment. Sadly, it is my duty to inform you of Cardinal Alberti's death, along with several others."

"I need details, Dr. ... Raison ... before I will continue this conversation."

"Understood, Madam President. My name is pronounced Reissen. Last night the department of Pro Deo was attacked by a vampire that your Lictor of Magic destroyed. Unfortunately, CMES was quick on the scene to gather its remains. This I witnessed. Within two months time, that vampire was resurrected and released to destroy as many sensitives, adepts, and witches on my staff as possible. Four were fed upon before I and two others destroyed the vampire again. And, I can assure you madam, that our incinerator properly finished the job. The creature's ashes are currently floating in a sealed vessel filled with the pope's own Holy Water. Is there anything else that you wish to know?"

"My God ..." was all that a near-speechless Silver Moon could say.

"Indeed, Madam President. I share your sentiments."

"Dr. Reissen, what can TIIIS do to assist your department?"

"Nothing immediately, but I believe, but cannot prove at this very moment, that CMES has played us both."

"I concur, Dr. Reissen. Shreds of evidence on our end have been building, and for what it is worth, we provisionally agree with your tentative assessment." Silver Moon stated with granite-like certainty as she vividly recalled her conversation with J.J. about a certain "priest" and a cleanup crew.

"Thank you, Madam President, for your willingness to assist at this time. However, I am at a loss as to how to proceed in a meaningful way. The Austrian in me wants to immediately call in an air strike on the CMES villa, while the humanitarian worries about collateral damage."

Silver Moon had to chuckle. This Reissen fellow was a straight-forward breath of fresh air.

"I have an idea Dr. Reissen. How about you settle into your new position, while my team brainstorms several appropriate responses? Then, once we have our act together, I will fly over to discuss them with you face-to-face."

"I like your style President Silver Moon."

"As I do yours Dr. Reissen. Let's keep in touch."

*   *   *

That evening, after Silver Moon flew on the company jet from Santa Fe to Latrobe, Pennsylvania, she arranged to have a late dinner with J.J., his wife Melaina, and an august member of the Old Oaks Academy faculty, Mr. Dexter, professor of magic and spells. Due to the short notice and the need for security, the foursome met in a corner booth of the Acorn, the campus pub in Old Main's basement. Here, low ceilings, lower lighting, intimate nooks and crannies, wooden beams and woodwork long etched with names and loves, wonderful food, and even better beer, all reigned supreme. Once the weekly hangout of Stone and his former mentor, the wizened Fourth-Class Adept, Mr. Henry, the place held many warm memories.

The foursome leaned in around a old church candle stub about three inches in diameter. Its flicker flame made their faces take on a ghoulish aspect in the poorly-lit atmosphere.

"So, Betsy, what's all the hush-hush about?" Stone wanted to know.

"Simply this, do you remember a certain conversation we had about a suspicious Roman Catholic priest?"

"Yes, what of it?"

"That priest, *and* the cleanup crew that arrived after you were finished, were all CMES."

"I knew it!" Stone said as he slapped the top of the rough-hewn table. Then he and Silver Moon filled in Melaina and Mr. Dexter on all the particulars.

"So we're sitting here to cook up some plan of retaliation?" Melaina summarized.

"Yes," Silver Moon said. "Options would be nice."

"I kinda like Reissen's idea of an air strike. That Austrian has the stones to do it."

"That's not constructive J.J." Melaina said.

"So," Silver Moon began the process, "what can we take away from CMES?"

"Another media smear campaign?" Melaina offered.

"Interesting idea, what else?" the president prodded.

"How about an EMP attack. Knock the hell out of their computers and communications." Stone replied.

"Again, an interesting idea. What else?"

Stone surprised Silver Moon with a question. "Why did CMES feel the need to revive that vampire in the first place? It had to have been a snap decision, a knee-jerk reaction to an unexpected windfall. So what motivated it?"

Gray matter turned round and round. Throughout the entire conversation, Mr. Dexter remained silent.

"They feel vengeful toward us for the victorious outcome of the Contest in the Alakrum Desert and the destruction of their Manhattan headquarters building. Even more vulnerable following the death-wish spell that wiped out their Rome headquarters," Melaina said.

"Do they know that we did it?" Stone asked.

"Very doubtful," Silver Moon replied.

"Feeling marginalized, that's their Achilles heel," Melaina concluded. "Everything points to their bruised ego."

Silver Moon smiled. "You know folks, you are downright dangerously creative people to be around. What if we somehow 'marginalized' their kind? You know, something like a *60 Minutes* exposé about them, their long history, and the composition of their membership?"

"In other words, to remove their curtain of secrecy?" Stone enthused.

"Precisely. And we marginalize them by pointing out, hey, they are nothing special, for here is the Vatican, here is TIIIS, and here are all these other covens, enclaves, and associations." Melaina added.

Silver Moon chilled the notion. "Such transparency would not sit well among our allies folks. No. It's their ego that needs serious bruising. So how do we do that?"

More silence.

"Well, for one, I am still hot about their use of our Lictor of Magic for their own designs. Bottom line J.J., we must find something appropriate that will let them know, *we* know, and we don't like it one bit," Silver Moon concluded.

It was then that the Frenchman, Mr. Dexter, unnecessarily raised his hand. He then explained his idea and boy was it a doozy.

* * *

While the four members of TIIIS were brainstorming away, an Austrian was reorganizing his life. First on his list, Reissen needed an assistant, so he approached Captain Abrams for a volunteer who could handle such duties. The military man grunted at the request, mumbled several choice words about the idea, and said, "I will see to it immediately, Dr. Reissen, but I make no guarantees. We are sir, after all, a dedicated security force." To his amazement several of his staff immediately stepped forward, eager to work side-by-side with "a vampire killer."

Now with an assistant, the Austrian, and Corporal Lucius Agave, began the process of removing all the blood-stained furniture and rugs from the suite. Frankly, it was grunt work, but Reissen felt that he needed it in order to make the suite his own.

"Corporal, I want all of this burned in the incinerator. I do not want one drop of that monster's blood to live on."

"Si professore!"

Two days later, after some serious housecleaning that found one near-mummified inhabitant, the pair moved in. Sheets of large-nub Pirelli rubber tiling were fitted to cover over the wooden flooring, while their work spaces consisted of secondhand gray steel desks and file cabinets. Reissen did splurge on the desk chairs, going for ventilated ergonomic designs. The only thing that the archaeologist changed to the suite's layout was his office door. He did not want one. And since the former one and its frame had been destroyed, it was a relatively easy modification.

Taking in their handiwork, the Austrian said, "Lucius, *now* I can work here." He turned abruptly to his assistant, "I need you to send an email to the forensic technicians and Pro Deo faculty. We need a meeting."

"When would you like to hold it *professore*?"

Reissen stopped and gripped the corporal by his shoulders and looked right into his eyes. "Lucius, for the tenth time, my name is Erik. Please use it."

"*Sì profes* … Erik!"

* * *

The first visitor to the newly-renovated Pro Deo operations suite was a man of the cloth dressed in simple white vestments. As he stood at the suite's threshold, everywhere he saw simplicity and efficiency. A young soldier with dark curly hair, engrossed with his laptop, was busy taking notes. Beyond him through a battered and unpainted opening in the wall, sat another member of the laity. This one had unruly black hair and also sat behind a simple steel desk. He too was busy working. The pontiff did not want to take them from their labors. As for the men, the cleric had already read their personnel jackets cover-to-cover. What he saw pleased him greatly so he quietly padded away, hands behind his back and head bowed in silent prayer for their future success.

Chapter 21

True to her word, President Silver Moon and her delegation of three paid a visit to the newly installed director of operations. One week later, the appointment, approved by the pontiff himself, was historic for never before had a member of the laity held the position. Certainly there were noses bent because of it—so the Austrian's sixth sense abundantly told him. He wisely chose to simply ignore it.

"How does it feel, Dr. Reissen?" Silver Moon asked.

"Heavy. Lots of paperwork. I fear for my research. But so far I love it. What do you have for me?" he asked opening his arms.

"Quite a bit of information actually, and a friendly suggestion as to how to appropriately respond to your neighbor's most recent machinations," TIIIS' president summarized.

"I see," the Austrian nodded, "but other than Mr. Stone here," the archaeologist emphasized with a roguish eyebrow, "who are these other people? Kindly introduce me Madam President."

"I would be happy to. To my right is faculty member Dr. Melaina Makris, professor of spells and an

Egyptian Demotic magical expert. She represents a long line of Coptic witches that reaches back to the fourth century. She is also Mr. Stone's wife."

Reissen simply nodded in greeting toward the exotically beautiful woman and remembered to carefully guard his thoughts.

Silver Moon continued, "To my left is *Monsieur* Lucien Dexter, who is also a member of our faculty. *Monsieur* Dexter is a Fifth Class wizard of extraordinary talent. He trained Mr. Stone, for instance, in the appropriate use of offensive and defensive magic. His suggestion as an appropriate response to your troublesome neighbor is the core reason why we are here today."

The Austrian nodded again in welcome, this time to the tall and thin Frenchman, with a measuring eye. He could literally *feel* the man's powerful aura emanating across the conference table.

"As for the man sitting next to you, Mr. Stone, our organization's Lictor of Magic, I believe that his introduction is unnecessary."

"Indeed," Reissen remarked, "his remarkable Texan accent has indeed preceded him."

"I think I have just been insulted," Stone said with a broad grin.

"Now, Dr. Reissen, we would like to tell you about our suggestion. *Monsieur* Dexter, would you please explain."

*   *   *

The Dexter Proposal, as it came to be known, was brilliant. Reissen knew without question that the late Sister Gabriella would have heartily approved. Best of all, the Austrian could not see any collateral damage caused by its implementation. But its global affect, now that *truly* represented a thing of beauty.

"There is only one small issue with the casting of this spell," Monsieur Dexter emphasized with one of his long and graceful fingers. "A witch of extraordinary energy and ability must perform the spell's casting. A male simply will not do." He finished shaking his head and pointedly looking at Stone's wife, Dr. Melaina Makris.

Without skipping a beat Makris said, "I'll do it. *Monsieur* Dexter, how must I prepare?"

"Your conjuring must expend your core energy as much as possible, for it is doubtful that the ley line nearby will accept your entreaty for cooperation."

"What sort of risk are we discussing here?" Stone wanted to know.

An exaggerated shrug followed by a wrinkled lower lip preceded the wizard's reply. "Difficult to say. But Dr. Makris is young and strong. She should survive the casting."

"Survive?" Stone breathed.

"Indeed, *Monsieur* Stone. One gets what one is willing to pay for."

At this point, Reissen rubbed at his chin in thought. Then, "This is a fine proposal. Like all such things, there are risks. I will move forward on the necessary preparations only after everyone around this table sleeps on this decision. We will adjourn and meet here again tomorrow morning at ten. Thank you for coming."

Once the TIIIS contingent left the conference room, Reissen remained. What concerned him most was placing another man's wife in potential jeopardy. That did not sit well with him. Then he thought back to his brash actions that led to the destruction of the vampire, Sigmund. Then, he had been single-minded, direct, and committed. The Dexter Proposal, in his mind no more than an embarrassing prank, had risk attached to it. Down deep it came to a decision of "yes" or "no." But he had already made up his mind. He would vote "yes."

CHAPTER 22

Later that very day, the Austrian had arranged to meet Dannica for lunch in a casual but nice outdoor setting. Their table sat beneath several pine boughs that richly-perfumed the area.

"Dr. Reissen, why the invitation?" the monster hunter asked.

"Partly I wish to thank you again for your assistance in addressing a difficult situation, and, partly to celebrate my promotion," the Austrian said while raising his glass of white wine. "A toast to the future."

After their sips, Reissen continued. "Have you ever considered working for a paranormal organization?"

The question, so directly asked, caused Dannica to stop and seriously consider.

"Dr. Ruthmann ... Dannica ... Astra, it must be lonely living between the two worlds—mortal and not. Please seriously consider my offer. There is *much* to learn and to share."

After several sips of her wine, Dannica finally responded. "I am truly flattered with your offer Dr. Reissen, but I have always been a loner. It is my way."

Reissen nodded in understanding and took a regretful sip.

"Just this morning," he began, "I met with four marvelous people from TIIIS. Do you know of this organization?"

"Yes, I do."

"Well, they came all the way from the United States to deliver a proposal for an appropriate action against CMES for their recent treachery."

"To bomb their villa into nothingness?"

"No. Their proposal was far more nuanced and subtle."

"So who are these people?"

A chuckle, "Dr. Ruthmann, you have already met one of them.

"I have?"

"Yes. Remember back to the first destruction of your father. Remember that thick Texan voice that warned us about the cleanup crew?"

"Why, yes. Yes, I do."

"Well, that was J.J. Stone, the TIIIS Lictor of Magic."

"Really. Why was he so difficult to see?"

"A special uniform that he wears."

"So no enchantment was involved?"

A head shake. "No. That was pure twenty-first century technological magic."

"Remarkable. So he was the one who bested CMES' champions in the Contest in the Alakrum Desert?"

"The very same."

Dannica became silent.

"What's wrong, Dr. Ruthmann?"

"That *man* killed my best friend in Barcelona," she firmly stated with anger in her eyes.

"Oh. What was this friend's name?"

"Portia Le Fey," the monster hunter said with a proud, upraised chin.

Reissen frowned, "Are we talking about the Elder Portia Le Fey of the Hidden Folk?"

"The very same," Dannica emphasized.

"Mein Gott!" Now with a building temper," Dr. Ruthmann, did you know that Elder Le Fey, in league with two other Barcelona coven witches, plotted to destroy a portal to the Underworld?"

An indifferent shrug.

"Did you know that I killed one of those witches in Egypt, while a colleague killed the other, thereby preventing their destruction of that portal?"

Now, a nervous sip of wine.

The fingers of his hand now angrily drummed on the cast iron table.

"Your friend, that *damn* Lictor of Magic, murdered my friend on her own balcony, in Barcelona," Dannica quietly hissed back. "What was her crime?"

Reissen's face went blank with shock and disbelief at Dannica's statement. "Le Fey only plotted to destroy the mortal world as we know it. Le Fey's list of atrocities is legion. Le Fey did not stoop to commit crime, she created outright horror. Dr. Ruthmann, do you know anything of her late husband?"

"She loved him dearly. She told me that often."

"No doubt. Still, he was the imperial inquisitor to the Sun King, Louis XIVth, and she, your good friend, assisted him in many of his imperial duties," the Austrian finished with a soft tone.

"And your friend," Dannica blasted back, "the much-vaunted victor at Alakrum, the Lictor of Magic, massacred the entire Barcelona coven. I know because I was there afterwards to see his bloody handiwork. I distinctly remember the smell of silver-ruined wounds, the long and deep sword cuts that sundered over sixty that awful night." Then Dannica leaned in, "Your Texas friend is an absolute butcher."

The Austrian took a final sip of his wine, carefully placed the empty glass down before him, and said to the indignant woman across from him, "Welcome, Dr.

Ruthmann … Dannica … Astra … *whoever* you want to be today. Welcome to the brutal realities of the paranormal world." He then took his wallet from his jacket, removed a twenty Euro note, placed it under his wine glass, and stood.

"Goodbye, my dear friend. Please accept my best wishes in your future hunts."

As Reissen walked away he felt diminished. He had truly wanted to recruit the dhampirica to his department. Believed in his heart of hearts such an experience would be of benefit to all. But that had been proven, oh, *so* wrong.

*   *   *

Dannica remained and coolly finished her wine. Initially, she wanted to throw it at the retreating back of that infuriating Austrian. So forthright, so smug, so … damn Austrian. Yet, so truthful. Dannica knew more about what Portia Le Fey and her husband Aubrey Rubin Le Fey had done than anyone, for Portia had revealed all to her. The two had argued endlessly about it. But in the end they had cried and lamented Aubrey Rubin's terrible demise at the hands of the Vatican.

As the monster hunter rose to leave, she had to admit that the damn Austrian was right—the paranormal world was indeed a brutal place. After all, she was a testament to that fact as a practiced monster hunter. Now with her father finally behind her, Dannica's agenda had cleared. She could now address some old business—revenge for the murder of her old friend Portia Le Fey. The dhampirica knew that her quest would be a difficult one, but she embraced it. To punish the TIIIS Lictor of Magic, Dannica would go to the States, and stalk him there.

Lo' unto them! For my vengeance will be the thing of nightmare.

CHAPTER 23

While the spell casting was straightforward enough, just doing it would be a challenge. The CMES-Rome headquarters, perched on that barren hillock, had its defensive lines in place since the first century. Hidden moats, trap doors, sally ports, and man traps were in place before the advent of modern video cameras with their overlapping fields of view. After the vampire Sigmund's string of attacks, the facility's head of security and communications added thermal imaging to the panoply. As far as CMES-Rome was concerned, they considered their defenses invincible to a direct assault.

*　　*　　*

The armorer at the Old Oaks Academy scratched at his shaved head. Before him on his laptop was a memo from his organization's president, Betsy Silver Moon. She made a request that was eminently doable—the construction of a special one piece UCS or Urban Combat Suit. The special provisions listed were not extraordinary. In fact, Mr. John Flynn liked them and immediately thought about incorporating several of them in Stone's next suit of urban armor. The extremely fit black man, with streaks of gray at his temples, sighed. Granted it would take some time, but his president's request would be honored. But what puzzled the expert fabricator was who was meant to wear it. Later that day, he found out.

"Dr. Makris, would you please stand upon this stool. And please mind your balance," the armorer said, betraying his accent from the southern hemisphere, as he held a hand to steady the witch.

Once in position, the six-foot armorer carefully draped a slitted muslin sheet over her head. Pulling the fabric this way and that until he was satisfied, Flynn began pulling pins from between his lips, pinning the sheet under Melaina's arms and along her general profile in rapid succession.

"How does that feel, Dr. Makris? Snug or loose?"

The witch wriggled some and declared, "Slightly loose."

"Good. Now, carefully as you can missy, slip it off."

Melaina did without displacing one safety pin.

"Wonderful. Now step down and take a chair. The tea over there is already on the boil, so make yourself at home while I whip this up."

"Home" was Mr. Flynn's fabrication shop, a close fifteen hundred square feet of well-organized work area complete with an electric forge in one corner, which explained the brimstone, ozone-like smell of the place. Everywhere tools and forms were on display—a well-used anvil with a set of hammers in a nearby wooden bucket, an English wheel stood near the bellows, and wooden benches bordered most of the walls upon which neatly-placed drawers filled with everything imaginable waited. In another corner a treadle sewing machine whirled as Flynn stitched the rough mockup together. Makris marveled at the man's amazing large-fingered dexterity.

Only halfway through her cup of Earl Gray, Flynn piped up, "Alright Dr. Makris, let's see how this passes."

After some wriggling Makris declared, "It fits like a glove Mr. Flynn!"

Smiling at the compliment, the New Zealander grunted with pleasure. "Now for the challenging bit— the fitting of your legs, feet, and headgear."

A week and a half later, Flynn invited Dr. Makris back to his shop, this time for a test-fitting. Several items were discovered during this session, but nothing beyond his abilities to remedy.

"Dr. Makris, kindly stop by my shop tomorrow at eleven. Then we'll button you up and put you through the paces."

*   *   *

Meanwhile, on the other side of the Atlantic at the Gregorian Museum, Sister Josephina Busby was hard at work. Her former teacher and mentor, the late Sister Gabriella, had performed a spell in Albania. Dr. Reissen, her good friend and colleague, had been there for the casting. It was Sister Busby's task to reconstruct it. The good sister had an edge as she, like Reissen, was an expert in Egyptian magic.

"So Erik, what do you think? Does this sound like what Sister Gabriella cast?"

After reading several melodious chants aloud, "Very much so Sister Busby," the archaeologist recalled. "Now all you have to do is come up with the necessary hieroglyphs to complete the spell, while I come up with an appropriate medium for its transfer."

*   *   *

Chairman William DeSalvo was disappointed. The vampire Sigmund's assault on the Vatican, based upon CMES' many and arcane sources—even some from within the Holy City itself, apparently had come to naught. The only satisfaction that the chairman had was one thin newspaper headline about a bomb threat. Thereafter, total silence and tranquility. Frankly, it vexed him. Such a perfect, deadly, deniable, and disposable weapon, *wasted.*

* * *

The forecast called for a blistering hot summer day. The weather forecasters made strong suggestions to stay inside and enjoy the air conditioning, or sit in the shade with a gelato. Just to make sure, the nondescript cab dropped off Dr. Makris in the residential area at high noon, and about two hundred meters away from her target.

As she silently padded along on her custom soft-rubber soled boots, the heat of the day did not trouble her one bit. In fact, the ventilation units of her UCS located over her kidney region just hummed along and kept her cool. Then the witch remembered Mr. Flynn's warning. "Be mindful, Dr. Makris, that no one can see you. Stay away from roadways, crowded sidewalks, and the like. Also, missy, your only hotspot is your evaporation units. Always face your target and they will never detect you."

The one-piece suit that the witch wore made her virtually invisible. Her passage could be best described as a totally inconsequential shimmer of a mirage, as the suit's fabric bent light and simultaneously reflected its surroundings. The bag that she carried over her shoulder was made of the same material, NSE, the inventor's humorous abbreviation for "No See 'Em."

Dr. Makris' suit was a one-off since Mr. Flynn had added another layer to its construction—one that foiled thermal detection. Further, the suit did not have any provisions for defensive weapons. The witch, if needed, would have to defend herself with her wits.

Not exactly happy about his wife's tactical deployment, The Lictor of Magic had already arrived on the scene suited up and fully armed in the unlikely event of an incident. From his place of overlook he had no idea where his wife was, a detail that he would later take up with Mr. Flynn.

"Melaina? Are you out there?" Stone whispered over his tactical radio.

A calm voice answered, "Yes dear."

"Where are you?"

"I'm in position, standing squarely in front of the villa."

"Oh."

CHAPTER 24

With arms outstretched as if in anticipation of embrace, the Egyptian witch sang a melodious song in her family's own ancient Demotic language. It was Dr. Makris' belief that the effort would only add to the effectiveness of the spell's cast.

> Life, life, life is to be again granted to this place.
> For too long it has been denied its place.
> *Wenet* and *Wenenu*, the favorites of green Osiris,
> *Wenet* and *Wenenu*, the fecund and abundant,
> Goodly *Unnefer*,
> He of 'Beautiful and Bountiful Renewal,'
> Breathe life into this place that has been denied for
> so long.

The witch repeated this long-winded chant thrice without blemish. When finished, Makris bent down and removed a beautiful male white rabbit, perfect in every way, from one chamber of her shoulder bag. It was the very Egyptian image of *Wenenu*. Then, she lifted out a female rabbit, *Wenet*. Around their necks were tied a white ribbon inscribed with the spell of renewal in hieroglyphs.

The witch gently placed *Wenet*'s and *Wenenu*'s magical *Doppelgängern* down upon the edge of the sun-scorched soil. Predictably, the rabbits began hopping forward toward the shade cast by the villa as their sensitive paws heated up.

Hop, plop.

Hop, plop.

Hop, plop.

The rabbits went and wherever their paws touched, a marvel of nature occurred. Long dormant life germinated. Spotty at first, each point the rabbits touched came to life and began to spread out like water dripped upon a paper napkin.

Smiling down and overwhelmed by this miracle, Makris turned around and left. The witch backtracked from the villa to her drop off point. But Dr. Makris could not help herself as she stopped and turned around to enjoy the rudimentary beginnings of a lawn filled with colorful wild flowers.

What Makris did not notice was the rabbits, now safely within the villa's shadow, nuzzling one another beneath a live security camera, quite out-of-range. Then, overcome with nature's own zeal, the rabbits began doing what rabbits do—the male vigorously coupled with the female. With every thrust and every contraction, magical procreative vibrations, oscillations, and tremors were sent throughout the hillock.

* * *

Alarm bells began ringing upon the detection of the rabbits' heat signature. They rose in intense urgency as the animals made their way closer to the villa's structure. Crossing over a weight sensor only added another alarm to the cacophony that now echoed throughout the subterranean bowels of the hillock.

A security technician on staff watched the approach of the tiny, long-eared heat signatures with curiosity.

"It's just two damn rabbits!" and reached over to override the hyper-sensitive alarm system.

But then, another heat signature appeared and the alarm system came to life again. This detection was truly odd—two circular signatures about four inches wide were moving away from the property about three to four feet above the ground. The technician had seen enough. He alerted the external security patrol to immediately make a sweep and inspect the villa.

Emerging at a jog from several sally ports, what the security teams found left them dumbfounded, their original orders long forgotten. The front slope of the villa facing the cobblestone lane was greening, and it was spreading.

*　　*　　*

"You did brilliantly!" Stone said to his wife. "And as you walked away for the exfiltration, you should have seen the faces on their security! It was like none of them had ever seen a green blade of grass in their lives."

"Why, thank you my love. That casting was perhaps one of the most meaningful things that I have ever done."

"Oh really?" Stone said with an upraised eyebrow.

"I do believe that I said 'one of the most meaningful things.' You, on the other hand, always will remain *the* most meaningful." as she pecked Stone on the cheek.

"Thanks sweetie. For a moment there, I thought I had been replaced somehow."

"Ah, my Lictor of Magic, you are irreplaceable."

* * *

The chairman of CMES Rome stewed in his cubical as he reviewed the surveillance video and its audio footage. Someone invisible had cast a spell upon his villa and then released some rabbits of *all* things. He now had lawns and gardens to attend to. The slight could only have come from one source—TIIIS. Only they had the technology to do it. As for the spell itself, that was pure Vatican. More a harmless prank than anything else. Nonetheless DeSalvo thought it an elegant snub to his clumsy deployment of a rogue vampire. The chairman could not have been more wrong.

*　　*　　*

The initial reaction of the life-giving renewal spell had indeed affected the immediate grounds of the villa. Its secondary effects took more time to take and soak in, for deep within the hillock a vast labyrinth existed of spaces, tunnels, chambers, and yes, even catacombs.

Within many of these places long-interred organic remains began rustle about. Those buried intact stirred in their places. For those not so fortunate, the plaster that imprisoned them began to crack and give way. Their bones often supported tunnel walls. Their skulls sometimes formed archways and convenient places for torches or electrical lighting.

The uncountable numbers included the tortured, the half-devoured, those buried alive, institutional dissidents, and the merely hated—not to mention troublesome witches, wizards, werewolves, wraiths, vampires, and ghouls by the score. These wretches represented centuries, lo' millennia, of CMES' safe storage of the great unwashed and unwanted. Those consigned to the blank inkiness of a forgotten pit with no name, by others who believed themselves better.

Unlike with the artless and technologically artificial revival of Sigmund, these wretches now tasted something rare and special—hope. They had been granted the breath of life again, which endued within each and every one of them a natural allegiance to something other than CMES.

*   *   *

But there is more, far more. Dr. Makris' casting contained a poignant irony. Years before, her husband, the Lictor of Magic, leveled upon this villa and its coven an automated death-wish spell that claimed many. Yet, CMES' resiliency allowed it to survive that plague of death. But this time, it would be the wife, a powerful witch, who would stun the Roman coven with … the gift of life.

CHAPTER 25

When Dannica finally arrived, at the Arnold Palmer Regional Airport in Latrobe, Pennsylvania, it was mid-fall. In comparison with her home airport in Barcelona—El-Prat Airport, the dhampirica thought of the facility as "quaint." And in many ways, it was. This "quaintness," however, Dannica thought appropriate. It so fit the TIIIS institutional persona of subtle camouflage and an unassuming presence.

The twenty-three-minute cab ride from the airport to the Old Oaks Academy's campus only reinforced the woman's opinion of this institution's abiding desire for maintaining a low-profile. Her cabbie even surreptitiously had to look up her destination's location on his GPS device before departing from the curb.

Upon arrival, they were in the middle of nowhere. The cabbie turned off the highway at the appropriately numbered exit. The otherwise unmarked road led off in a southerly direction, and hidden away behind a copse of old oaks, stood a solitary limestone archway of monumental size. This massive and squat construction looked totally out-of-place, isolated the way it was. But Dannica recognized it as a scaled down version of the Arch of Titus in Rome—an arch built in his memory.

"Would you please stop under the archway?" Dannica heard herself saying.

"No problem, ma'am. I'm kinda curious about it myself."

Getting out of the vehicle, Dannica walked over to its front and craned her neck in the brilliant morning sunshine. The workmanship was extraordinary. All the carved details along the roof's architrave, the mid-level horizontal border, and periphery of the arch were crisp and clean, although weathered gray. In the broad field between the architrave and mid-level border appeared the Latin words—*triumphos adversus malum lux*—"light triumphs over evil" in large oxidized bronze letters.

Then the vampire hunter noted that the interior of the arch was inscribed as well. While the left side remained blank, the right was anything but. At the top *In Memoria* could be easily read from the deeply carved stone. Beneath that title appeared name upon name arranged in horizontal rows. Clearly the top-most rows were the oldest based upon their weathered condition. Before each name was added a symbol indicating their religious affiliation—the Christian cross, Judaic Star of David, Crescent and star of Islam, the swastika of Buddism, Jainism, and Hinduism, and the ying and yang of Taoism. Their sheer diversity amazed her. For she could not assign anyone that she knew in the Barcelona coven to any of them. The first name of those listed, however, struck her as strangely familiar. As for the last four rows midway down the field, all were freshly carved.

"Seems that quite a few died quite suddenly," Dannica murmured to herself, a thought that immediately resurfaced the Barcelona coven's massacre and the reason why she had traveled so far—vengeance.

Before getting back into the cab, Dannica noticed the date on the arch's keystone, it read simply "MDCCCXV."

Once again inside the cab's warmth, she asked the cabbie, "Who is James Madison?"

Startled by the question, the he blurted out, "Why that's the fourth president of the United States. Why do you ask?"

"His name is inscribed on that monument."

"You don't say."

*   *   *

What Dannica did not notice were the arrayed security cameras hidden on the internal and backside of the entranceway's arch.

"Charley, check this out."

"What Pete?"

"We have a visitor, and from the looks of her, she must be some sort of a European model. What do you think?"

"Yeppers, you're right, Charley."

"I wonder who she is here to see?"

"Maybe a new student?" Pete hoped.

"Naw, for some reason I don't think so. Do me a favor Pete, run the plates on that vehicle."

"Already have. They are owned by AAA Cabs out of Latrobe."

"Huh. That probably makes her from out-of-town. Maybe even Europe."

"You've got quite an imagination Charley."

"Yeah, still, let Abigail know she's coming her way."

"Will do. But I'll bet you a quarter that she's headed for the Sandströme Building, instead of Old Main." Pete goaded.

"You're on!"

*   *   *

Once past the archway, the roadbed gently ascended a field of a mowed emerald green lawn framed by a gaily painted fall oak forest. Dannica could not help but draw the comparison between this lushness and the stark barrenness of the CMES-Rome headquarters.

After driving some distance across the vast mowed expanse, the road crested at a rise that overlooked the Old Oaks Academy's campus. The view was so striking that the cabbie stopped his vehicle to take it all in. Immediately Dannica was smitten by the sheer beauty of the setting. Nestled within a grove of Pennsylvania old growth forest, a ring of structures stood framed by leaves painted in brilliant reds, oranges, and yellows. Through its center ran a broad stream. A looping pavement connected them all.

"Miss, which building do you want me to drop you off at?" the cabbie asked.

Looking down at her notes Dannica answered, "Old Main."

Descending from the crest, the cabbie consulted a road sign with arrows that pointed this way and that. He made a right turn onto the looping pavement.

Since its inception in 1812, the Academy's campus had expanded far beyond Old Main's cathedral-like solitary tower and its cruciform foundation. On this day, Old Main's thick limestone walls are encircled by magically augmented structures, each constructed in their own architectural style, whether Egyptian, Greek, Romanesque, Gothic, or Bauhaus aluminum, glass, and steel. And indeed, the cabbie had to wind his way around them to reach Old Main's imposing front entrance steps. Along the way, placed in prominent locations, clusters of students tended freshly tilled gardens in preparation for the coming spring.

Dannica paid the man's fare, tipped him handsomely, and exited the vehicle's warmth and once again confronted the sunny mid-morning chill. Wearing a dark gray slack suit with matching overcoat, she came prepared for the weather. Even so, her breath left a vapor trail over her right shoulder. Several ascending steps later, the dhampirica pushed at one of Old Main's heavy wooden doors, but before she did, Dannica noticed the Latin engraving around the gothic limestone portal. Reading it she realized, *That's quite a defensive spell!*

Then she saw another cornerstone, this one said "MDCCCXIII."

* * *

"That quarter is mine!" chortled the security guard. Only a slight grumble came from the other.

"So Charley, do you think she saw the camera as she scanned the defensive wards?"

"Naw, that sucker is in the eye of a gargoyle. Not a chance."

*　　*　　*

Once inside Old Main, a wall of heat greeted the vampire hunter, but did not prepare her for the open spaciousness supported by dozens of lofty rosette columns. Immediately, the expanse reminded her of the sacred and hushed interior of the Cathedral of the Holy Cross and Saint Eulalia in Barcelona. The only thing missing was the scent of frankincense. With her footfalls echoing off the stone pavement into the distance, Dannica approached the long oak receptionist desk to her right. Behind it sat a middle-aged woman with an invitingly bright green aura that almost matched her beaming smile. Her lapel name-tag said, Abigail Watts.

"May I help you dear?"

"Yes, please, Ms. Watts. My name is Dr. Dannica Ruthmann. I am from the University of Milano. I wish to know where Mr. J. Stone's office is. I have just arrived and wish to surprise him."

Watts took in this lengthy overture. The receptionist listened carefully to the stilted British accent and her mind began to churn. Nodding, the woman consulted her computer screen.

"Mr. Stone's office is located on the second floor of Meyers, office number 203. Are you new on campus?"

"Yes, quite."

The receptionist stood up to peer over her desk at Dannica's feet. "Ah, good, you're wearing low heels."

"Why …"

"Because the narrow and winding staircases over at Meyers are a bitch to climb in heels."

"Ah, now I understand."

"Alright then," Watts continued, "I will make a map for you," the woman said as she began drawing with a yellow magic marker. Once finished, she placed it before Dannica.

"Meyers is two buildings down on the right." She helpfully pointed while pushing the map toward the visitor. Then she paused in thought and said, "Allow me to check his schedule."

After some moments, "Yes, as I suspected, he is in lecture now."

"Might I ask where?"

"In Meyers, Lecture Hall B, on the first floor. You can't miss it. It faces the building's entrance."

"Thank you so much. One other thing, if you do not mind. Why are all those young people fussing in the dirt? Are they growing their own food?"

Smiling broadly, "Those 'young people,' Dr. Ruthmann, are our students. And no, those garden plots are strictly for flowers. Come next spring, by early May, they all will be judged. Winning the Spring Flower Contest is a big deal around here."

"Are there any rules?"

"Only one—absolutely no magic can be employed. Only Mother Nature can be involved."

"I see. How wonderful. Thank you again, Ms. Watts."

And Dannica moved on, but not before making quite an impression upon the receptionist. For Abigail Watts, a Second Class Adept herself, had never before witnessed a dull silver-gray aura tinged with red in-the-flesh. Curious, she looked it up and found that the combination did not exist in the usual Chakra listing. It was only then that she realized that the visitor's thoughts had been completely blocked from her as well.

So far, Dannica's impressions of the TIIIS campus were beginning to shake her resolve, make her question why she was really here. The Barcelona coven and CMES were nothing like this place, so full of life and helpful people.

In comparison to Old Main, Meyers turned out to be a medieval fortress built of red sandstone in the best Romanesque tradition. Built low, wide, and stout, the structure had narrow and highly defensible gateways and arrow slits for windows, even with iron gratings. Again Dannica took note of the Latin inscriptions that ringed the entranceway with another defensive spell. This building's cornerstone said "MDCCCXV," the same as the archway.

Once inside, warmth greeted her within a narrow stone passage that led to a central gathering area. There students milled about or sat along the perimeter on low stone benches. To her dhampirican eyes, they appeared like a sea of brightly glowing auras, so full of youthful energy, exuberance, and … happiness. Not one were of a muddied or darkened shade.

Stopping in the center, she scanned the area, and saw the entranceways to lecture halls A through C. She entered B's and found herself in a passage lined with coat hooks and nooks, almost all were occupied. It was only when she nearly reached its end that Dannica heard a deep and resonating male voice. She stopped at the corner of the passage to eavesdrop, unseen.

"I'm sorry, Ms. Albert, but magic cannot be so categorized, and in such a blithe manner. All the systems that you mentioned on Wiki are just modern attempts to organize something that itself defies organization. Magic, at its core, is an intimate relationship between a practitioner's innate ability and training, and the environment. It is a practitioner's will and intellect that bends the environment to a specific goal or purpose.

"In short, you cannot discard *The Knot of Eternity* just because you happen to think it's message is antiquated, insensitive, or sexist. In fact, I challenge you to find a more respected and authoritative source. And that is precisely why all of you received a copy of it on your first day of classes, because is the best, most concrete view we have of our multiple realities. Even our most bitter opponent, CMES, recognizes that fact, and studies the document stem to stern, even though their own coven's foundation predates *The Knot of Eternity*'s composition by over a millennium. They, CMES, recognize the document's value, and its sober encapsulation of the dark, light, and mortal realms."

Dannica just stood there speechless. Never before had she even heard such a lucid explanation of the subject. And not once did her ears hear any hint of a thick Texan accent. *Was it possible that there were two Stones on campus? It's a common name.*

There was only one way to find out. She made the turn around the corner and entered the lecture hall.

*   *   *

Stone stood in the lecture pit looking up at his class of Demonology 101 students. He thoroughly enjoyed speaking in the acoustically perfect, semi-circular, wooden amphitheater. Even his whispers could be distinctly heard in the top-most row of seats. Consequently, the Lictor of Magic saw any physical movement within that field of view as well, especially the late addition of a striking woman with long black hair in a gray pant suit, who now sat up high and to his left.

Almost immediately, the First Soul came alive in his head. *Soul carrier! Beware! She is a dhampirica bent on your destruction! Gird yourself for battle!*

At the stern warning of impending doom, Stone just stopped his oration and stared. Almost immediately, the audience of two hundred and five turned to look at what had caught their lecturer's attention. The effect was as if a searchlight's beam had been focused upon the newcomer. Unaccustomed to such exposure, Dannica crossed her long legs and belligerently stared back at Stone, daring him to do something untoward.

Turning away, Stone continued, "Are there any other questions about the validity of *The Knot of Eternity*?" but when he glanced back at the intruder, his heart skipped a beat as the woman in the aisle seat, somehow, now sat six rows closer.

Soul carrier, the First Soul warned again, *she is about to spring at any moment!*

Stone took heed, calculated her distance at twenty yards, and purposefully turned sideways to her, while he held several defensive spells at the ready.

Again turning his eyes away, Stone spied a raised hand. "Yes, sir. What's your question?"

He first saw it out of the corner of his left eye. The overhand throw was brilliantly timed and executed.

Stone, in response, made time slow.

At the glittering blade tumbled in the air toward his head, he waved aside the flickering weapon with a subtle psychic push of his left hand, and it struck noisily upon the slate blackboard behind him leaving a shattered crater.

Almost simultaneously, the woman threw two shiny star-shaped objects underhand. Their flight bracketed where he stood, so the Lictor of Magic didn't move, which took courage. The one on the left he again pushed aside, but the other cleanly sliced through most of his right ear. Blood flowed from the sensitive organ. He ignored it. Both missiles also crashed into the black slate behind him, and ricocheted once before they embedded themselves into the wooden floor.

*   *   *

Seeing that her weapons had failed to reach their target, Dannica *moved* on the figure bathed in a blindly bright platinum aura.

Using her seat as a springboard, the dhampirica flung herself through the air, down toward the pit, where her prey stood motionless. With arms fully extended and nails ready to strike, Dannica herself became a missile fueled with blind revenge and bloodlust.

*   *   *

Soul carrier! The First Soul screamed into his inner ear.

Stone couldn't believe what he was seeing. Here was this attractive woman, one who he remembered last with Erik Reissen in Rome. Now the same woman, for reasons unknown, was literally inbound. From the look on her face, she was prepared to tear his throat out, if not his eyes as well.

In response, and not a nanosecond too soon, Stone thrust both of his open hands at the woman. All that Stone registered was her echoing scream of *"BUTCHER!"*

The impact of the Texan's double bolt of psychic energy not only stopped the dhampirica in midair, but then violently propelled her back into her seat with a bone-crushing crash. Still holding his arms forward, Stone waited a beat, saw his attacker's lolling unconscious head and sagging form. Only then did he relax to take out a handkerchief from his jacket's breast pocket and cover his much-damaged right ear. Blood had already soaked the right side of his white Oxford collar and the lapel and shoulder of his favorite tweed jacket.

His audience sat transfixed during this drama, all with large O's for mouths. Snapping them out of it, he tersely ordered, "Will someone please call the infirmary? We have someone seriously injured."

Then he thought to add, "And it's not me."

*   *   *

After twenty-three stitches to his right ear, the emergency physician carefully wrapped up her handiwork, transforming Stone into a swami.

"You were quite lucky, Mr. Stone," she chided. "Another couple inches to the left, and you would have lost your eye."

"Thank you doctor, for that cheery message," Stone grumbled back.

"She only has your best interests in mind darling." his concerned wife Melaina said from across the crash cart.

"Thank you, doctor. This time I mean it."

"You're most welcome, Mr. Stone. Would you like to visit your assailant?"

"You bet!" Stone said, while attempting to stand up. His wife steadied him. "Hold on there, partner. Are you good?" she asked.

"Thanks. And yes. Lead on doctor. I have a boat-load of questions for that woman."

Only some forty steps away in a guarded private room, lay the assailant, restrained, with oxygen, a fully wrapped torso, and a saline drip.

"Doctor, what am I looking at?"

"I really don't know Mr. Stone. Her aura is all wrong. Her metabolism is elevated. Her blood work is off the charts. Her DNA—who *knows* until that comes back from the lab. She suffered five broken ribs, a damaged sternum, and one hell of a bump on the back of her head, which my money says she'll feel the most. And by the way, she has been listening to this entire conversation. She's now fully conscious and playing possum."

"You don't say doctor?" Stone said. Now walking up to the patient's bed railing, he challenged, "Just who the hell do you think you are to barge into my lecture? And then attack me!"

Two bloodshot eyes sprang open blazing with hatred, pain, and defeat.

"And just what the hell do you mean by calling me a 'butcher'?"

A dry, gravelly voice answered, "Because you are!" As Dannica strained against her bonds. "You butchered the entire Barcelona coven. I know." Her lip curled." I witnessed your carnage. Their wounds reeked of your silver sword."

Now wheeling toward Melaina, "And you were his accomplice in the horrific murder of my friend Portia

Le Fey!" she screamed from the bed. "I saw you enter and leave her flat. It was you who covered her body in holy salt!" Only then did the dhampirica sag back into her bed.

After several moments of silence, Stone asked reasonably, "Do you have any idea what the Barcelona coven did, consistently, for centuries? And as for Le Fey, what about all the atrocities that her husband and she committed?"

"Portia was my friend. As for Aubrey, he was a true monster. Even so, he did not deserve what the Vatican did to him."

"I see." Stone said with his hands on hips. "So because Le Fey was your friend, she deserves a pass on her attempted destruction of the Netherworld's Gate."

Only silence came from the one bound to her bed.

Stone turned to the aghast physician, who couldn't believe what she was hearing. "Doctor, how long before her wounds heal?" Stone demanded.

"It's difficult to say. Her metabolism is so different. But maybe, two to three weeks."

"What are you anyways?" Stone pointedly interrogated the patient.

Dannica answered with pride and an upraised chin, "I am a dhampirica."

Returning to the physician, "What do we know about them?"

"Next to nothing. They are extremely rare. But now we have blood-work and DNA. That's a start." She concluded with a shrug.

"I will not remain so bound for two to three weeks," Dannica firmly announced, "I heal fast, but I need fresh liver to speed my recovery."

"Do we have that in the commissary?" Stone asked the doctor.

A nod, "I suppose."

"Then get her all the liver she can eat."

Looking down on his assailant, Stone asked, "If I get you released, are we good?"

A shrug.

"*THAT WON'T DO DHAMPIRICA!*" Stone bellowed. "I want your word that you won't go on another vendetta rampage."

Locking eyes, "You have my word, Lictor of Magic, with one condition."

"What is it?"

"That at your next lecture, you explain to your class *why* I called you a butcher."

Without any hesitation Stone replied, "Done."

*　　*　　*

The next day, after having gorged herself upon fresh livers, Dannica's X-rays revealed no fractures. Her sternum had miraculously repaired itself. As for that knot on the back of her head, the doctor's bet paid off and she signed the woman's release papers.

* * *

That same day, Stone, with his head elaborately bandaged, entered a packed but hushed Lecture Hall B with a lot on his mind.

"Ladies and gentlemen, it's time for a come to Jesus moment. Two days ago, you witnessed lethal combat, firsthand, within this very hall. As proof," he turned to circle the three craters in the blackboard in white chalk, "as if you need any," now pointing to his head, "I was attacked by a very rare entity called a dhampirica. If you don't know what that is, look it up. But for the moment, put down your devices," he paused with an upraised finger, "I request your undivided attention."

Stone paused to gather his thoughts. He stood before them at attention and with his hands behind his back.

"Put bluntly, but frankly, the world in which we live is a dangerous one. You saw that first hand two days ago. In this world nothing is black and white—instead you will encounter nothing but an endless series of gray gradations. Don't like that? Well, tough luck, buttercup, that's reality, and that's the reason why you are in my class, because demons never play fair.

"Two days ago, you heard my assailant call me a butcher. She was absolutely correct in every respect. Full disclosure: several years back, I butchered an entire coven in Barcelona. By my own count, over sixty individuals and outright demons died by my hand."

Stone paused to let that sink in. The silence in the lecture hall was deafening at his admission.

"As Lictor of Magic, it is my sworn duty and responsibility to protect the innocent and destroy evil. By anyone's standard, including CMES', the Barcelona coven was a renegade enclave. Its reputation for carnage forced CMES to remove them from their membership in the mid-nineteenth century. They were that much of an embarrassment to *their* reputation. I was asked, not ordered, to take them out. I was presented with a window of opportunity. I took it, and I did so without regret."

"And that, ladies and gentlemen, is today's lesson. Because nothing, absolutely *nothing* in the paranormal world, is black and white."

*   *   *

Unknown to Stone, a quietly crying woman listened in from outside the lecture hall. Years beyond count, filled with self-doubt, fear, anxiety, and hatred had been stripped away in seemingly an instant. While she cried about many things—mostly about her utter loneliness and many poor choices, Dannica also sobbed for this Lictor of Magic, far more teacher than butcher, who had remained true to his promise. And to his brethren, who had only shown her respect and good will.

ABOUT THE AUTHOR

For W.J. Cherf, this is his third leap into the realm of paranormal archaeology, mixed with a dash of magical fantasy and contemporary science fiction. His first book of the Adventures of Paranormal Archaeology series, *The Magician's Tomb*, brought screams of delight from his passionate readership. *Netherworld's Gate* brought gasps for the who-done-it and why.

Cherf is no novice to either archaeology or the ancient world, having excavated in Israel and Greece, along with extensive travel throughout the length of Egypt. Ask him sometime about what a sunrise looks like from atop the Great Pyramid. Or for that matter, walking ancient roads and surveying precarious mountain fortifications in Central Greece. Even better, inquire about a certain Fourth of July celebration atop Tel Beer Sheva in Israel.

As to why Cherf writes in his retirement years, he says, "I always wanted to write a book without footnotes." While this is surely true and is an oblique reference to his treadmill "publish or perish" days in academe, more than that drives the man. On more than one occasion, Cherf has said he has all of these stories in his head, which bedevil him until freed upon the world. In the end, you decide.

For free chapters of Cherf's works, not to mention a handy source for the latest and greatest in Egyptology, go to www.wjcherf.com. Cherf always says, "Sample before you buy." For reviews, go to www.amazon.com and search under "w.j. cherf." If you like this book, review it there. That's how authors find out if they still have the right stuff, straight from their readers.